FALL QUARTER

FALL QUARTER

BY WELDON KEES

✤

EDITED AND WITH
AN INTRODUCTION BY
JAMES REIDEL

STORY LINE PRESS

1990

The editor would like to express his gratitude to the
Bennett Martin Public Library, Lincoln, Nebraska

⟡

Library of Congress Catalog Card Number:
90-52856

ISBN: 0-934257-43-4

Book design by Lysa McDowell

Published by Story Press, Inc.
d.b.a. Story Line Press
Three Oaks Farm
Brownsville, OR
97327-9718

BOOKS BY WELDON KEES

POEMS

The Last Man (1943)
The Fall of the Magicians (1947)
Poems 1947-1954 (1954)
Collected Poems (1960)

FICTION

The Ceremony & other stories (1984)
Fall Quarter (1990)

CRITICISM

Reviews and Essays, 1936-55 (1988)

LETTERS

Weldon Kees and the Midcentury Generation (1986)

BEHAVIORAL SCIENCE

Nonverbal Communication (1956)
with Jurgen Ruesch

WELDON KEES AND *FALL QUARTER*
AN INTRODUCTION BY JAMES REIDEL

Two days after Pearl Harbor, in Manhattan, the editor Paul Hoffman recommended to Alfred A. Knopf that he reject Weldon Kees's novel *Fall Quarter*. In Hoffman's reader's report, the sobering reality of America's entry into World War II looms over the small, personal setback for the young poet and fiction writer who worked in the Denver Public Library:

> It may be that last night and this morning were not precisely the best times to read a light novel about campus life in the Middle West, but if my reaction were even only half reliable, I'm glad we made the sort of contract we did. Because I'm very much disappointed in the book. Instead of turning out to be a "tart, amusing tale given just a tinge of seriousness by its irony" as it promised in the beginning, it seems to me to have turned out a bad caricature. At first I thought things I objected to were merely lapses in discrimination and began to make notes as cuts and revisions but as I got into the new text, I gave up. Every one without exception behaved more and more like a screwball and presently even the properties, so to speak, of the piece began to take on a look of incongruity.
>
> But it is entirely possible that as I began all this by saying, I chose the wrong time to read it.

vii

Six days later, Hoffman's colleague Harold Strauss was in agreement, reacting with undisguised rancor:

> Kees has not only botched the job completing this novel; he has also revised most injudiciously the part which we had already tentatively approved. Indeed, revised is too mild a word, for he has ditched the previous chief female character, who was quite an amusing screwball, and substituted for her a very ordinary gold-digging wench. Not only is the new female much less interesting, but the best part of the narrative structure had been undermined. I am entirely in accord with Mr. Hoffmann that we should let this go.

Kees received a letter from Hoffman on the day after New Year's Day, 1942. The dismay of the readers' reports was not translated into the politesse of a typical rejection letter. Instead, Hoffman reported to Kees with the same brutal honesty that he did to his boss:

> I'm being so candid with you because I think you would want me to be. And I want to say here that I think Miss McIntosh [Kees's literary agent] is entirely right in wanting you to put this book away and not try to sell it elsewhere. I'm almost willing to wager that its publication not only wouldn't do you any good but might hurt your future chances [...]

Hoffman is quoted in Kees's letter of January 3, 1942, to Norris Getty, an Army lieutenant whom Kees befriended several years before when both were editors for the Nebraska state guidebook compiled by the WPA's Federal Writers Project. Kees tested his new work on Getty and provided him with a front-row seat on his career, filling his frequent letters with reportage ranging from literary gossip to getting his work in print (always a brief, unpretentious entry), and the vicissitudes of dealing with publishers (always dealt with at length). "I don't know," wrote Kees. "What do you make of all this? Are these people completely humorless and dense, or is the book really bad? I don't think so, and from the way you wrote, I don't think you do either. But Jesus, Norris, I just feel as though I'd told my favorite joke and nobody even smiled."

The story of *Fall Quarter* needs what anything written about Weldon Kees requires, that is, a story about him, for Kees is hardly well-known outside of those who are familiar with his poems—often the only medium in which his achievements are encountered. As one of his editors said, the poet Donald Justice, "One of my pleasures in reading Kees has always been 'I knew the work of this poet and you didn't.' That sense of private discovery...is the source of my continuing interest." In the case of Kees, biography must figure into any discussion of those achievements. For unlike other literary figures of his generation, the virtuosity of Kees's cultural life should be seen as a whole as well as have its components examined individually. He must be considered not only a poet, but a fiction writer, a critic, a visual artist, a filmmaker, a photographer, and a jazzman. Profiled in *The San Francisco Examiner* in 1951, Kees impressed the reporter as a "poet-artist" who "refuses to limit himself."

It would not be inappropriate to say that his greatest triumph as an artist was the creation of an artist whose different vocations, triumphs and failures are inseparable. In one man's career is the cultural history of the midcentury. The three volumes of poetry Kees published before he disappeared in 1955, presumably committing suicide by leaping off the Golden Gate Bridge, the scattered paintings, short stories, the lost novels, and other works Kees did in search of the avant-garde spirit, should be seen as a whole.

The publications and events that have reclaimed Kees's works mirror his diversity. This reclamation began in 1960 with the publication of Stonewall Press's *The Collected Poems of Weldon Kees*, edited by Donald Justice. There followed, over a twenty-year period, two paperback reprints, anthologies, a handful of articles and elegies by younger poets moved by Kees and the tragedy of his short life.

Collections of Kees's fiction appeared in 1983, first

with the special supplement that Timothy Nolan and I assembled for *Columbia 8*. Later that same year, the fine press edition of *The Ceremony and other stories* by Weldon Kees was published, selected and introduced by the poet Dana Gioia, and later expanded for the trade edition published in 1984. Both selections reveal a side of Kees that has been in neglect since the early 40's.

In 1986, The University of Nebraska Press published *Weldon Kees and the Midcentury Generation: Letters, 1935-1955*. This volume, with commentary by its editor, Robert E. Knoll, surveyed Kees's life and work, showing the full range of his interests as well as providing a documentary portrait of the cultural world and personalities of his time. Kees's letters are as intriguing as his poems. They are, in a way, the swan song of the art of letter writing.

Over the past decade, the first books appraising Kees's contribution to literature and the visual arts appeared. *Weldon Kees: A Critical Introduction*, edited by Jim Elledge, put together virtually every piece written about Kees, including previously unpublished essays and a bibliography of Kees's poetry, fiction and criticism by Bob Niemi. And William T. Rowse's *Weldon Kees*, a critical monograph in the Twayne series of American writers, became the first book-length study devoted to Kees.

Reviews and Essays, 1935-55 by Weldon Kees appeared in 1988, a book for which I selected critical writings that Kees did for *Time, The Partisan Review, The Nation, The New Republic, The New York Times* and other publications. In that volume Kees's severe and discriminating criterion is shown in some of his finest writing. In the reviews of novels, poems, art exhibitions, films and popular music, it is possible to see Kees's modulations from fiction to poetry, his interests in abstract expressionism and the whorehouse jazz of the 20's which he wanted to revive. Also present is Kees as a gifted "dilettante" in the vanished sense of the word, a renaissance man who would have been at home in the 16th century rather than the 20th, the man described in one of his celebrated Robinson poems as a "confidant of Popes."

In February 1988, at New York's CDC Gallery, a painting and collage by Kees were included in an exhibition of the Irascibles, the eighteen artists whose boycott of a Metropolitan Museum exhibition of modern American painting in 1950 became a cause célèbre in the history of American art.

Both as a respected art critic and a painter, Kees contributed to the debate that resulted in the establishment of the abstract expressionists as representatives of the avant garde in America, a triumph personified by the famous group photograph of the majority of the Irascible 18 published in *Life* in 1951. Unfortunately Kees was not in the photograph, and his reputation as a visual artist did not benefit from the public attention that made artists like Robert

Motherwell, Jackson Pollack and Mark Rothko household words. Nevertheless, for the first time since
1955, his work has been exhibited alongside that of
his New York School colleagues.

In the autumn of 1988, a symposium held in his
hometown of Beatrice, Nebraska, brought together
many of the poets and scholars who have written
about Kees. It was also during this event that a handful of Beatrice dinner-theater actresses performed something entirely different from their typical repertory
of light comedies and musicals. They brought to life
Kees's one-act, existential play "The Waiting Room"
in the dining room of a Best Western Motel. It was
the modest world premier of a play that had not
been acted since its rehearsal in May, 1955, when
its intended first performance was canceled by the
San Francisco fire marshall.

The publication of *Fall Quarter* provides an opportunity to see Kees in the role of a novelist, a
vocation he pursued with the most commitment from
1935 to 1941, when he tried to publish at least three
different novels.

Born on February 24, 1914 in the small railroad
and manufacturing center of Beatrice, Nebraska,
Weldon Kees was the only son of John A. Kees, the
owner of a factory that produced ice and roller skates
as well as other die-cast metal products, and Sarah
Green Kees, a woman who would not have been out

of place in Grant Wood's "Daughters of Revolution," who could trace her lineage back to the *Mayflower*.

Early on Kees showed a precocious interest in writing and presenting his work to others. On his father's mimeograph machine, he turned out his own magazine which he filled with stories, verses and drawings. With his cousin, the children's book writer Bernice Wells Carson, Kees published what was for both of them their "first" book, a handmade pamphlet titled "Imbiciles" which contained limericks and cartoons. These childish pastimes matured into a youthful commitment. At the age of fourteen, Kees reviewed early talkies he had seen on a trip to Minneapolis with his father writing criticism for *The Beatrice Sun*. From that time on, he never abandoned writing criticism until his disappearance in 1955.

As would be expected, Kees wrote for his high school paper and was also a member of the drama club. It was probably as a teenager that Kees developed the eclectic and voracious reading habits evinced by his knowledge of literature and his rather encyclopedic capacity for subjects ranging from Henry James to strange diseases and sedatives. Arcanum abounds in his writing, and it did in conversation that was "like his poetry... apt to consist of apparent irrelevancies" according to the memoirist and novelist Janet Richards, "which he could bring all together [so] you felt like you had just glimpsed the grave."

The restlessness of Kees's migrations from city to city, and from one vocation to another, first appeared during his undergraduate years. In 1931, Kees entered Doane College, a small, Presbyterian institution in Crete, Nebraska. From there Kees transferred to the University of Missouri, taking courses in English and Journalism, finally matriculating at the University of Nebraska in Lincoln.

There Kees came under the influence of the editor of *Prairie Schooner*, Lowry C. Wimberly. With his encouragement, Kees began to write short stories for *Prairie Schooner*. The first, "Saturday Rain," was published in 1934, and was listed as one of the "Distinctive Short Stories in American Magazines" in Edward O'Brien's *Best Short Stories* volume the following year. As Kees began to regularly place short stories in *Prairie Schooner* and other magazines, he felt confident enough to turn to novel writing. The first was *Slow Parade*, a manuscript now lost. In August 1935, he described the novel to his college friend Maurice Johnson, while summering in his family's cabin in Colorado:

> I'm working like hell on this novel, trying to get it finished before the summer is ended. And it terrifies me a little because there always seems to be so damn much more I want to put in it and I know now that there are some things in it already that I don't want: things that must come out; but perhaps it will amount to something and some people will like it and at any

rate it isn't anything to be ashamed of: yet [...] And
so I work from five to eight hours a day on a screened-
in porch with the river flowing by making rainsound
twenty feet away, with pines behind me, with the
typewriter on a stand I made out of a peachcrate [....]

I am working with a technique that is similar to Dos
Passos', but in one sense his method inverted: where
he (and Charles Dickens) take isolated characters and
bring them slowly closer and closer to each other,
I'm trying to take the members of one family and
show them growing farther and farther away from
each other. I hope that you'll be able to read it in
MS. before the final draft: [...] there is a greater need
for criticism before books are published than after.
(Vide: Thomas Wolfe.)

Words like "rainsound" show Kees was reading
Joyce. Indeed, his letter displays the self-assurance
and informed uncertainty of a young writer working on his first novel. Surrounded by the benefices
of an edenic setting, he was aware of the masters
from whom he had borrowed, and whose influences—
both good and bad—he must rebel against in order
to accomplish something new.

In the autumn of 1935, Kees abruptly stopped taking graduate classes at the University of Chicago
and left for the entirely different milieu of Los Angeles. During the Depression, the film industry was
in its golden age. Hollywood was an attractive al-

ternative to the conventional job market for talented
young people who had heard about the fantastic salaries actors and screenwriters were making. This aspect of Hollywood was especially apparent to Kees
because of the success of the actor Robert Taylor,
who was from Beatrice, and whom Kees had known
as Arlington Brugh since childhood. Their acquaintance, however, did not help Kees find the screen-
writing work he was looking for in the winter of
1935-36, a time of flux when he quickly learned that
Babylon did not appeal to him:

> I stayed two days in Hollywood with the Beatrice
> contingent and was more than happy to escape. Merely
> call to mind all the wild stories you've ever heard-
> about that mad and terrifying region, augment them
> with recollections of all the satires about it, and that
> is the actual and genuine Hollywood. Ben Hecht's
> remark, to the effect that out here they're all "either
> drunk or crazy" is fairly accurate ...

While Kees observed the dissolute side of Holly-
wood, collecting impressions that appear in his short
story "Do You Like The Mountains?" and the novel
Fall Quarter, his letters kept friends up to date on
Slow Parade as the book made the rounds of New
York publishers:

> Covici turned the book down. Three of the men there
> wanted to publish it, Straus[s] and some other per-

son didn't. From Harold's letter—I'd like to have your
reaction to it: "... We have been forced to come to an
adverse decision, however, on the score that in the
last analysis you do not dig deeply enough into the
psychology of the four children. You tend to describe
them as types in broad terms which would fit hundreds of similar characters and you do not work down
to the special flavorsome qualities of the individual.
..." Special flavorsome qualities, indeed! What do you
think of that? My own feeling is that while they may
be what Mr. Strauss calls "types," people today seem
in a broad sense, to fall into such classifications. To
be anything but a type you have to be Thomas Wolfe
or something like that.

Surely Emma Bovary is a type; so are Studs Lonigan
(there are thousands of him), Babbitt, the people of
Dos Passos, Hermann, Caldwell. Or am I wrong? [...]
At least there has been no uniformity of opinion on
Slow Parade from those who have read it. Covici at
least had the good grace to say nothing about it being
"unrelievedly grim." It's at Vanguard now. I still
have much hope for the book.... Now working away
at notes on a new one, *A Good American*; and a novelette,
The Dead Are Friendly.

Kees returned to Nebraska in the summer of 1936,
and found a job with the Federal Writers' Project
editing material for the *Nebraska State Guide*. Despite
the benefits his friendship with Norris Getty had
for his writing, Kees found his stint with the WPA
to be dull and to have little renumeration save for a

few appearances in Federal Writers' anthologies.

He took courses in the summer of 1937 at the teachers college of the University of Nebraska. These endeavors, paradoxically, must have at once seemed the correct path for a writer who needed a source of income—for even in the late 30's, it became apparent to American writers they could not support themselves by publishing alone. And given his later years, Kees was not adverse to using a classroom or lecture-hall setting as a platform. In Provincetown in 1949, Kees led symposiums on cultural issues like poetry, painting and popular music. He was a lecturer at Robert Motherwell's abstract expressionist "school," Studio 35, in the Lower East Side and at Berkeley in the early 50's. Yet, as with Chicago, after a few weeks of education classes, he was left bored and disaffected again with the idea of teaching, a disaffection apparent in *Fall Quarter*. In the following description of the novel's hero, Kees denies an idealized future in the teaching profession as he affirms it with a naive voice that has a more subtle irony than Harold Strauss found:

William Clay's academic successes had made it easy for him to find a position. His future seemed assured. He would teach freshman English for two years in the university of a nearby state, as his contract specified, saving as much money as he could for work in the East on his Ph.D. On completion of his doctorate, he planned to marry Frances Hyatt, a girl from his

home town. These next two years of teaching, he hoped,
would be full and productive. He planned to write
several articles for the scholarly journals.

Kees planned to write novels. Yet having not sold
a manuscript meant supporting himself in some way
that would give him the existential elbowroom to
be a writer. If there was something to be had from
William Clay's formula for a well-tempered life, it
had to facilitate being an artist. And Kees found this
in his marriage to his small-town girlfriend, Ann
Swan, whom he had known since his senior year at
the University of Nebraska.

Kees found in Ann a helpmate who would for sixteen years support his ambitions, being for him anything from an editor to a drinking companion to a
source of income when Kees needed to devote himself entirely to his creative work.

Her letters that survive reveal wit and intelligence
remarkably similar to her husband's. She sometimes
referred to herself and Kees as a "family." But they
were childless—unless you consider the poems, novels,
paintings, and other works substitutes for offspring.

They were married in Denver on October 3, 1937,
a few months after Kees had left Nebraska to a degree in library science at the University of Denver.
He was also able to find a position in the Denver
Public Library, where he eventually became the acting director of the Rocky Mountain Center for Bib-

liographical Research, a government-funded project to establish a union catalog for the libraries of the region. The position surrounded him with books and periodicals, a natural environment for Kees. And it did not interfere with his writing.

In *New Directions 1937* there is anthologized a Kees short story that may resemble the mood of the lost novel, *Slow Parade*. "I Should Worry" begins with the precondition of a double suicide, that of the parents of an alcoholic car parts salesman who sells his deaf, broken-armed sister for enough to buy a drink. The film noir quality, the presence of a morality compromised by the economic duress of the Depression, shows the risks Kees took to write fiction with a kind of numbing social commentary, and to differentiate himself from the then-popular romanticism of Thomas Wolfe and his imitators. This desired effect to shock, however, resulted in a book that was meeting the obstacles in taste and mores Kees sought to challenge.

After going from house to house for over two years, *Slow Parade* was warmly received by Doubleday Doran. Eager to be a published novelist, Kees took a tactical step backward and agreed to revise the salacious content of the original manuscript. He wrote of his willingness to "consent to minor changes if it would get the book in print" in a letter to Getty, dated January 23, 1938, and then shared with his friend a

long passage from the first letter sent by Doubleday
Doran's editor Donald Elder to show that being
compliant could yield more than one contract:

> Your book has had several readings, and everyone
> has been unqualifiedly enthusiastic about it. I've never
> seen a first novel get such a hand as yours has and I
> think we're going to publish it. However, there is one
> obstacle which prevents me from making you an of-
> fer immediately. DD is a very conservative house, and
> it has a long established policy of strict censorship. I
> don't agree with the policy at all, and if I had the
> authority, I wouldn't hesitate to publish Slow Parade
> as it stands. But since it's a house policy that I can't
> do anything about, I have to take it into considera-
> tion. It is with some hesitation that I make this propo-
> sition to you but if you would consent to making some
> changes to enable the book to pass the censorship
> requirements without weakening it, I think that we
> can work out a very satisfactory contract this book
> and for future ones.... The part which requires change
> is Cynthia's sexual aberration [and] a good deal of
> the dialogue which doesn't meet the purity standards.

In the same letter to Getty, Kees condenses the
waiting game of practically having his book accepted, of being told that contracts were in the mail,
and of being informed that *Slow Parade* was turned
down because "the book couldn't be adapted to con-
form to the policy of the firm." Elder continued
with what little comfort he could offer: "I can only

congratulate you on joining a very distinguished group of modern American writers whose books have had similar luck at our hands."

Kees sent the manuscript on to Viking, and *Slow Parade*, as a topic for his letters, disappears as he exchanged it for other projects. Elder's concern over the character Cynthia is as much as we will know about the content of Kees's first novel. It is something to be guessed at—like the fate of its vanished author.

During the summer of 1938, Kees wrote Getty about how happy and encouraged he was producing new work:

> ...I've written two sketches (additions to the growing library saga), a long story with a dance-band background, and one or two other unfinished things [...] most important of all, to me is that I've got most of a long section of a new novel finished. For the time being the book is titled But Not The City, and will consist of four long sections, one laid in the equivalent of Beatrice, Western Nebraska, one in Hollywood and Los Angeles, one probably in Chicago, one in Lincoln. Getty, I've written and rewritten this one part eight or nine times, and have had great pleasure from each revision. Ann likes it better than anything I've done and so do I. When I'll finish it I don't know. When I get stale on it, I fool around with that never ending tour de force The Crowd, to be completed in

1945 or thereabouts. But I promise you it will be a
fair book. It is pretty complex in scope but confines
itself to one character in whom irony and pity are
equally mixed. I hope. Yes, you're right, when you
do a novel you get more depth or whatever—even
though I distrust such words.

It is difficult to determine how many novels Kees
tried to write based on his correspondence from the
years 1938 to 1941. Working titles were sometimes
revised. In late November, 1938, Kees mentions to
Getty that his new novel is "now titled The Days
And The Years." And in her letter of December 9,
1940, the author Mari Sandoz wrote Kees to give
him her approval of another lost novel: "I am pleased
with Passage. It has sensitivities and the lucid prose
of your short stories, which you know I have always liked." Sandoz, the author of the best-selling
memoir of her pioneer father, *Old Jules*, resided in
Denver during the time Kees worked in the library.
She had known Kees since his days as an undergraduate at Nebraska, and her success made her an
important advocate for Kees.

Given one of her comments, Kees had become frustrated by his failures with the New York publishers: "There seems only one way of accounting for
[Passage's] meanderings among publishers," Sandoz
wrote, "—its location in a pre-war world."

Kees's imagination, however, was absorbed by the
immediate conditions of social and historical stasis,

the torpor of the late Depression/isolationist America that was about to disappear. Although Kees does treat the subject of isolationism in *Fall Quarter*, the threat of war seems remote in the novel, complementing the period and geography Kees wished to capture. It was a time and place where nothing happens, a point of twilight in history that did not hide from Kees the meaninglessness of life; the nail Kees would pound over and over again, especially in poems like "For My Daughter" and the Robinson sequence. Perhaps to deny or even defy Sandoz on the direction of the public's taste, Kees titled the novel that precedes *Fall Quarter*, *Nothing Happens* to make his subject insistently clear.

As a kind of talent scout for Alfred A. Knopf, Mari Sandoz provided Paul Hoffman with enough intelligence about Kees to warrant a closer look at the promising young story writer. In his letter to Sandoz of January 7, 1941, he informs her that the west coast representative for Knopf was going to "look up Welldon Keyes [sic]." And in a matter of weeks, Kees sent his New York agent Mavis McIntosh the first nine chapters of *Fall Quarter*, which she turned over to Knopf in February, 1941, under the working title of "Spring Quarter."

In the new novel, Kees stayed inside the loose autobiographical parameters he had set for himself in 1938, parameters he had already used to shape the lost novel *Nothing Happens*, in which a danceband musician struggles to the a writer. "I would stick entirely to 'known' material," he had written Getty, "things that have happened to me, things heard, seen, etc. Principal character: an approximation of myself. (You can't write about yourself, really; try it; it's impossible.)" Using his still fresh observations of campus society and, perhaps, a desire to excoriate himself for contemplating an academic career (or Norris Getty and Maurice Johnson for their ambitions to be teachers), Kees wrote a send up of the schools he attended.

In Paul Hoffman's initial reader's report to Knopf, Kees's formula for an academic farce was an improvement over a book on the previous year's list:

This is a novel of life in a western college town, more specifically of one William Clay's. He is an English instructor of 25 who has just arrived on the scene, having only the previous spring taken his M.A. back home somewhere in the mid-West. Filled to the brim with the usual idealism about and enthusiasm for his exalted calling, his is the old story of pretty immediate disillusionment and discouragement. However, the book does not by any means confine itself to Clay's academic life but is rather his whole personal story as well.   Which is an amusing one, since he is at the beginning anyway pretty much of a stuffed shirt. Infinitely better, I think, than GEESE IN THE FORUM —although not, except occasionally and secondarily a satire as that book is—I found it good reading and would like Mr. Strauss to have a go at it.

Unlike Hoffman, Strauss, when he was an editor
at Covici, had been exposed to Kees's social commentary and the deliberately cardboard stereotypes
that populate his novels and stories. This may have
been the reason why Strauss, in his reader's report
to Knopf, was more vigilant about weaknesses in
Fall Quarter:

> I think that there are reasonable grounds for follow-
> ing Mr. Hoffman's suggested procedure, i.e., give Kees
> a contract that is to become operative upon accep-
> tance of complete MS. We can do this in good faith,
> for I should say that chances are we shall want to
> publish. The story has sincerity and bite, and moves
> right along. It is not by any means an important book,
> and at times I found the irony (which is Kees' chief
> implement) a bit heavy-handed. Nevertheless, the central
> character, with his fatuous idealism and his jarring
> disillusionment, is very real, and Kees has an excel-
> lent eye for odd details—the offensive Peke, for in-
> stance, who sheds yellow mange powder on the board-
> ing-house carpets, and the mannerisms of a gent who
> is the author of "The Boys Book of Camera Craft"
> and thirteen similar opera. For the fact is that the op-
> pressive life of the college town drives the inhabi-
> tants to cherish their idiosyncrasies (to put it mildly).
> If you live long enough in this kind of atmosphere,
> you begin to take the screwballs for granted. When
> Kees does that, he is amusing. But sometimes he
> "protests too much." He becomes dogmatic about
> things that should be left to the reader's intuitive grasp.
> That is what I mean by "heavy-handedness."

The only other flaw I find is that for the page-and-one-half following p. 83 Kees suddenly switches his means of perception to Janet Eliot. The rest of the story is told through William Clay's eyes, this brief passage is a disturbing interruption. What is more, it is unnecessary, for the developments disclosed in the passage are, or can be, made clear elsewhere.

But the book looks as if it will turn out to be a tart, amusing tale given just a tinge of seriousness by its irony. I can't offer a comparison with GEESE IN THE FORUM but I recognize that here is a divestation of the moribund conventions of faculty life.

Despite the sardonic realism and the strange, Punch and Judy-like handling of the characters, there was nothing to indicate Kees was being disingenuous with the genre of an academic farce. The Knopf people could detect little to be chary about in the early chapters. They believed Kees would follow some kind of formulaic pattern. After all, the first part of *Fall Quarter* seemed to be business as usual: a book that might turn a profit and shore up the more serious literary titles the Knopf house prided itself in, a book that might even be turned into a motion picture starring Fred McMurray. But the novel is instead more like the German film *The Blue Angel*. William Clay's infatuation for the radio chanteuse Dorothy Bruce is as precipitous as Professor Rath's for the cabaret performer Lola.

Fall Quarter is indebted to Evelyn Waugh's *Decline and Fall*; however, references in its content and the jump-cut pace reveal the influence the movies had on Kees's writing. The novel's characters share a superficiality that is no deeper than the stereotypes of Hollywood. When reading *Fall Quarter* today, one can quickly identify the madcap of the novel with that of old B film comedies—or such "serious" fare as *Reefer Madness* with the wild parties and drugs. There is, however, something calculated in the insignificance of the characters, and something more in the "heavy-handedness" Strauss saw in Kees.

Even if the characters in *Fall Quarter* were not directly taken from the cinema comedies of Kees's day, they originate out of the same archetypes the Hollywood scriptwriters utilized: the young professor, the demimonde, the drunk, the society girl, and bohemians fixed in the popular imagination. In Kees's novel, however, these characters are not just figures of satire. They are the parodies of parodies shopworn even by 1941's standards. Kees, who would write in a 1944 review of Preston Sturge's *Hail The Conquering Hero* that in "a farce, a character forced to play a role that humiliates and torments him is sure to arouse high merriment," subverted this not-so innocent process. Humiliation and torment go unrelieved in *Fall Quarter*. Kees destabilizes his light comedy with the unrelenting appearances of cruel children and the frequency of adverbs like "hysterically" and "futilely" to describe a dystopia in which William Clay and the other characters are dehumanized inhabitants: coequals of the dogs in *Fall Quarter*—those foils of the Thin Man's Asta and American dog worship in general.

Kees did not "like" the characters of *Fall Quarter*, showing little of the genuine affection that most novelists have for their creations. Kees's are the engines of his disdain for them, teratological renderings that differ markedly from the preciousness of the sensitive and sympathetic portraits of Randall Jarrell's *Pictures from an Institution*, a roman à clef based on his years of teaching at a women's college.

In that novel, set in the relative security of the 50's, Jarrell gently satirizes with intricately woven descriptions and dialogue. They all come off, as he intended, like harmlessly affected and slightly overgrown children: habitués of an eastern, liberal, progressive school surrounded by nothing more disturbing than the Republican-controlled Senate. For Kees, however, the characters of *Fall Quarter* have been dropped into their maker's relentless opéra bouffe, where they behave like lapsarians in benighted times.

Knopf sent Kees a contract following the recommendations of Messrs. Hoffman and Strauss. In Hoffman's letter to Mari Sandoz of March 21, he thanked her for her discovery: "You were a good girl for putting me on to him."

Through the spring and summer of 1941, Kees worked on *Fall Quarter*. During that time, there were anthology appearances supporting the view that only good things came from the young Denver librarian. And they were not missed. Sandoz noted to Hoffman in her letter of June 28 that Kees was "pleased over his dedication in the O'Brien." It was an honor that would look like good dustjacket copy to the Knopf editors, and it would have flagged something a little more substantial about Kees, something they were not getting about his metier.

Kees's debut contribution in 1941's *Best Short Stories* was "The Life of the Mind," a dark portrait of a vaguely homosexual and anti-Semetic college professor. To those who had followed Kees's fiction, this was the latest installment to his insistent analysis of the commonplaceness of inhuman behavior. And with the story's affinity to the novel in the sharing of a campus setting, there was enough, even at the most superficial level, for the Knopf editors and Miss McIntosh to have stopped to take a look at what would have possibly temporized their expectations of Kees's academic comedy, for the same agenda that operates as pathos in "Life of the Mind" operates as bathos in *Fall Quarter*'s devolution into the absurd. Unfortunately they expected ordinary fluff from a man who had written the following in the poem "Early Winter," printed in *New Directions 1941*, an annual publishing professionals watched:

an annual publishing professionals watched:

But the room is cold, the words in the books are cold;
And the question of whether we get what we ask for
Is absurd, unanswered by the sound of an unlatched door
Rattling in the wind . . .

Although poetry had not replaced fiction in Kees's growing canon, he was devoting more and more time to verse in 1941. Increasingly it was getting into print —enough, evidently, to impress Paul Hoffman. In a letter to Getty, dated July 8, Kees wrote optimistically, on a first-name basis even, about what he thought would be a long-term relationship with someone he thought respected his work: "Hoffman says Knopf would be very much interested in a book of my poems; so we will hope he's right. Since Paul is more or less in charge of the selection of poetry at Knopf's, the chances are pretty good."

Kees's speculation about a first book of poems shows ambition of the poet was eclipsing that of the novelist. In another letter to Getty, dated July 31, there is the presence of just such a transition in the voice of a writer going through the motions: "This is Thursday, my day off, and I've been working on the novel most of the morning. The last few pages sound like Jos. Conrad at his most labored and there is no pleasure in it for me."

In August, Kees betrayed more impatience with the burden of completing *Fall Quarter*. The need to finish it before Getty was transferred overseas was a priority as America's involvement in the war became more certain:

> It's not likely that I'll have a clean draft of the novel typed before the end of September, and the time you suggest for your reading will be fine. It isn't quite done; my letter must have given you the wrong impression. But the end is very near. I have been fiddling with this manuscript for so long I don't know what to think of it any more. Without the interest and encouragement of you and Ann, I'm sure it would still be in the 100-page state. I'm not forgetting the Knopf "encouragement."

Kees believed he could count on Norris Getty to find things wrong with the novel in the eleventh hour before sending it to New York. If Kees was apprehensive, it is hidden somewhere in his mood as he handed over the manuscript on October 28, described in the letter he wrote Getty in faraway Fort Huachuca, Arizona: "A gloomy little man from the Railway Express people has just gone out carrying the MS. of *Fall Quarter*: I hope it reaches you soon. It would be fine if it would arrive in time for you to cope with it over the weekend. I know you're rushed like everything, but I'll be awfully grateful for any and all reactions and suggestions."
Within days, any fears Kees had about his burnout affecting the text of *Fall Quarter* were dispelled

by his friend:

> Well, the misgivings are quite resolved now, so there's
> no harm in admitting them. They were largely, I can
> see, the result of reading so much of the book piece
> by piece, over so long a period of time. Yesterday,
> Saturday afternoon, I read the whole novel through
> at one sitting. Under pleasant conditions, too: got up
> from a nap about four, showered, got out the manu-
> script, and settled down by a west window, with a
> good view of peacefully autumnal mountains at my
> side, and week-end quiet (wonderful thing) in the
> barracks. It was after dark when I finished, and I felt
> much pleased with the work, went out to the China-
> man's for supper in quite tranquil frame of mind. Tell-
> ing myself, as I have told you here, that I should
> have trusted you more all along. [...]
>
> Your weather is handled beautifully throughout, and
> helps the book a lot.

Getty had only a few minor reservations, one of
which concerns the Mrs. Oatley section. Getty told
Kees: "You really shouldn't have taken her out of
Hollywood. That was where she belonged, she had
a whole chapter to relax in, getting boozy as she
pleased; and the whole atmosphere was far more
intimate, with the hero himself playing the piano."
Getty's disappointment is proof that Kees had ap-
propriated characters and scenarios from an earlier
novel, probably *Nothing Happens*. If this was a habit

of Kees, it would support the idea that each of Kees's novels were built on the ruins of a predecessor and that *Fall Quarter* is fairly representative of the lost novels.

On November 6, Kees responded:

> Your letter came yesterday and I read it over a couple more times this morning before I settled down to make changes on the ms. [...] I was awfully pleased that you liked the book. I thought all along that I was writing a "well-made" novel in spite of steady doubtful feelings, too; I think I have and hope I'm right. [...] Your suggestions were fewer than I expected, which was all right, too; I have acted on most of them. [...] Now I don't want to write anything for a while, except some poems, perhaps.

Buoyed by Getty's reading, Kees sent *Fall Quarter* to Mavis McIntosh the next day. There was nothing in Getty's letter to dissuade Kees from how he had finished the novel. Naturally, it was a total shock to him how his agent and the Knopf editors reacted. And in the aftermath of the rejection, Kees held nothing against Getty even though it was Getty who sanctioned what the Knopf editors felt had "botched" *Fall Quarter*. In Getty's letter of November 2, he had written: "The cutting of the Janet Eliot episode to its present length seems to me all for good—necessary, in fact. As it now stands, the episode is just a build-up for the Dorothy affair; it gets William's mind started away from Frances, without stealing any thunder from Dorothy, and that is just what it ought to do."

It took three weeks for Getty to write something to soften the blow of *Fall Quarter*'s rejection. The routine of Fort Huachuca had been transformed by the declaration of war, and Getty reported that he was "Busy as all hell" with the black troops he was training for combat.

He was the first to apprehend how the two Knopf editors had miscast, if not underestimated, Weldon Kees as the author of light reading material; but Getty was at a loss to say why the novel that worked for him had not for others. On January 24, 1942, he replied to Kees:

I would have written before, somehow, except that I find myself kind of speechless before the ways of publishers; like two-headed calves, they inspire in me a degree of disgust, but no very intelligent comment. There's no sense in any of it, so far as I can see. I mistrusted the beginning of the novel, for reasons which were largely corrected in later drafts, but I liked the whole. Apparently their reactions worked in exact reverse. Just what the devil they thought they were getting to start with, I cannot imagine. What they mean by "changing heroines" I cannot understand at all; you were almost pedantically careful, I thought, in getting your heroine introduced at the very beginning. In short, if only it were not so very important, and so sharp a disappointment, it would be one of those things just to shake your head over and forget.

Looking for other opinions to confirm or contradict Paul Hoffman's, Kees informed Mari Sandoz of his rejection in January and allowed her to see the manuscript. Although her reaction to the novel and its rejection, in her letter to Hoffman of January 17, is certainly not an apology ("I had a hilarious time with it, even took the manuscript along to dinner with a professor"), nevertheless it forced Hoffman to acknowledge the possibility that he and Strauss had missed something: "maybe we're all wrong—and for [Kees's] sake I hope we are—but we just couldn't see the book at all."

In the fall of 1941, Kees's first book of poems, *The Last Man*, had been accepted by the Colt Press, a publisher like the Cummington Press, known for its elegant, hand-printed editions of modern poetry. The long wait for this book's appearance, delayed by wartime paper shortages, became the focal point of his literary career during 1942 and 1943 whereas the placement of *Fall Quarter* would become more and more a sideshow for Kees. But in the months following its rejection, after Mavis McIntosh ceased to represent him, Kees tirelessly sent the book to different publishers to prove the Knopf people wrong.

It seems, however, that editors who read the novel during the war years found the same reason to send it back. In a letter to Getty, dated March 29, 1942, Kees wrote:

Colt is not taking on anything else just now—too many books on the fire, I guess; so I sent FALL QUARTER to Duell, Sloan & Pearce. Today this came from Cap Pearce: "I wonder if your novel, FALL QUARTER, isn't one which must be regarded as a casualty of the war. We all find it most readable but at the same time think that there are strangely unreal moments to it and that the chances of its making any real appeal in these times are slight. Maybe our outlook is too dominated by the war and its many gloomy and challenging developments. But since four of us who read the manuscript came independently to pretty much the same conclusion, we have to follow our best judgment and decide against publishing your book. At the same time I would like to say that there is no doubt in the minds of any of us about your ability to write exceedingly well. Maybe some day we will have a chance to see another ms. of yours, etc, etc, etc, etc, etc."

In June of the same year, an editor at Harper & Bros. reiterated the effect the war was having on the reception of *Fall Quarter*:

It's a damnable fact but nevertheless true that there are fashions in books just as there are in women's clothes; and we [...] feel that a novel making a sophisticated analysis of college life would hardly stand a chance if published today. The war is partly responsible. You may have noticed, for example, that almost all the books listed as best sellers today are in some way related to the war, and the same shift in public interest holds right down the line.

As the war became more and more painfully self-evident as the obstacle to *Fall Quarter*, Kees gave up placing the novel on his own. While at Yaddo, the artists retreat in Saratoga Springs, New York, in September, he reported to Getty that he had "picked up a new agent, Russell & Volkening. They seem to go in for screwballs: they handle Wyndham Lewis and Henry Miller and Eudora Welty, and like writers to be a bit off-the-beam. Time will tell what they're really like; but they do have senses of humor and do like *Fall Quarter*, which they have now at Scribners."

Ann and Weldon Kees separated for unknown reasons in February, 1943. There is little to explain the estrangement, only the silence Kees requested of Getty ("Please say nothing of this.") in a letter informing his friend he was bound for New York. The separation lasted for several months. Then, just as mysteriously, Ann rejoined her husband.

New York was the natural place for a young writer to be close to publishers and to the milieu that he had thus far only associated with during prior visits, his summer at Yaddo, and through his energetic correspondence. Practical reasons also contributed to his relocation. His library project lost its funding when the last Depression-era programs were superseded by the war. And there was Kees's anxiety over

being drafted. He had assembled an anthology of
satiric verse, and induction jeopardized its chances
of publication if he had to wait for answers to his
inquiries from a Denver mailbox.

During the war years, Kees supported himself by
writing reviews for *Time* and continuity for Para-
mount's newsreel service. Poems (that would in 1947
comprise his only trade book, *The Fall of the Magicians*) had replaced novels and short stories. In November, 1942, he had confessed to Getty:

> I've written no fiction in months; just don't seem to
> have the vocation any more. Or perhaps a clue may
> be found in this passage, from Hemingway's intro-
> duction to his anthology of war stories: "The only
> true writing that came through during the (last) war
> was in poetry. One reason for this is that poets are
> not arrested as quickly as prose writers would be if
> they wrote critically since the latter's meaning, if they
> are good writers, is too uncomfortably clear."

A few weeks after Kees had arrived in New York,
Fall Quarter is mentioned for the last time in a letter
to Getty dated March 21, 1943. Some kind of cultural malaise Kees ascribed to the wartime patriot-
ism, and his growing disinterest in writing fiction,
made the novel a dead issue:

> Scribner's were on the verge of accepting FALL QUAR-
> TER when Henry Volkening had it there a few months
> back, and when I told them the idea for another novel

I want to write (when and if one can think of such long-term projects again), they reopened the case for FALL QUARTER. But yesterday I heard they decided no on both books.... Another publisher is "interested" in both books, but then, everyone is "interested." You know. The writer may be drafted and do another Pvt. Hargrove. Do you agree that that young man should be thrown to the lions, along with Pvt. Saroyan? It is really getting quite bad.

The synopsis for a novel among Kees's papers and the handful of last short stories placed in obscure magazines during the war years represent a strange combination of ambition and ambivalence Kees had towards his fiction. In the synopsis, he shows like he does nowhere else how he consciously imagined scenarios as black-and-white films, and how a novel in 1944 for him was the means for making the next *Citizen Kane*. It led to nothing; however Kees did bring the synopsis to life as a kind of nightmarish fantasy of a Kees biographer, for it is mysteriously prescient about the Kees who would contemplate a new life in Mexico before his disappearance eleven years later:

> Carl Ellis, a young scholar at somewhat loose ends, comes upon a volume of poems by a writer named Fredric Shore Strandquist. Fascinated by his work, which is little known, Ellis attempts to find out something about Strandquist, with a view to writing about him, but meets with small success [...] After following several roads that turn out to be blind alleys, Ellis dis-

covers that Strandquist's family lives on Long Island, and goes out to see them.

[...] The story from then on will deal with the progress of Ellis's search (which takes him to Chicago, San Francisco, Hollywood, Denver, and several small places in the middlewest and, finally, back to New York again), in the course of which he comes in contact with many people Strandquist has known, including two of his wives and several mistresses. He learns that Strandquist twice changed his name, is a bigamist, may be a murderer, and worked at a variety of occupations, at some times making fantastically large salaries and at other times living in great poverty. The more material Ellis assembles, the more confused he becomes as to what sort of man Strandquist was: he seems to have been capable of many changes of character and personality. Ellis's quest is further complicated by the fact that he suspects persons who knew Strandquist are lying to protect themselves.

Ellis's discovery that Strandquist is still alive, and his meeting with him forms the climax of the book, with Strandquist's personality at last fully clarified for the reader, if not for the man who has searched for him— for Ellis has seen and heard too much and knows that the task of fully discovering and understanding another human being—at least this one—is an impossibility. A moving picture version would of necessity, I should think, concentrate on the shock effect of Strandquist's appearance and the contrast between his expected personality and "real" one. The whole work, I hope, will have the same kind of chase excitement supplied by Greene and Hitchcock.

While living in New York and Provincetown during the remainder of the 40's, and in San Francisco from 1951 to 1955, Kees established himself as a poet. And he filled the vacuum left by his abandonment of fiction, turning to abstract expressionism, working in collage, oils, and gouaches, and writing art criticism for publications like *The Nation*, where he had replaced Clement Greenberg.

The only real interest Kees had in fiction during this time was assisting Anton Myer with his first novel during a time when the author of *The Last Convertible* was trying to emulate Malcolm Lowry and James Joyce. Although it was in no way a collaboration, Kees's correspondence with Myer shows an enthusiasm that suggests Kees delegated to Myer a role he had missed out on. Kees gave Myer's first novel its title, *Evil Under the Sun*, and he is a model for one of its Provincetown art colony denizens. He also contributed lyrics to the text because Myer could not afford the royalties to quote authentic popular songs. So closely was Kees tied to Myer's book that he reacted with as much emotion to good and bad reviews as if he had written the novel himself.

Kees's involvement with Myer resembled that of a seasoned novelist. Yet Kees had not published a novel. And his enthusiasm for *Evil Under the Sun* did not reawaken the urge to write a new novel or to rework the manuscripts of the novels he had already written. Instead, if an uncorroborated story is true, Kees in 1952 or 1953 burned what he said were his unpublished novels in a kind of mock ceremony for Myrer and his wife at that time, the painter Judith Rothschild. This would seem to be true given that all of Kees's novels are lost except for *Fall Quarter*, the survival of which can be attributed to the encouragement of Kees's agent, Henry Volkening.

Since 1943 the novel had been on the periphery of Kees's mind. Then in the fall of 1951 he contacted Volkening after not having engaged the agent for some time. Kees needed Volkening to personally intercede on his behalf to dislodge the manuscript of his third book of poems languishing at Harcourt, Brace. Evidently, Kees had been submitting the book, titled *A Breaking and a Death* (published as *Poems 1947-1954* by the printer Adrian Wilson), to trade houses on his own without success. It was in Volkening's letter that informed Kees of the rejection of his book of poems that the agent brought up *Fall Quarter*, offering to submit "that old old novel by one Weldon Kees."

Over the next four years, Volkening pleaded with Kees to reconsider the novel. In May of 1952, he replied to a letter from Kees that must have had nothing but scorn for the earlier dream of publishing *Fall Quarter*:

I've taken upon myself to mail you the manuscript, rather than to follow your drastic advice that I should throw it away. For though after you look it over you may want to do this yourself, there's just a chance that you still see in it what you once saw, and what I still see: a publishable novel which sadly no one has thought to be so.

Volkening's faith in the novel, and his patience, held up to Kees's rebuffs during the last phase of Kees's life, when he atomized himself into cultural ventures that filled the increasing silences between poems, silences that must have fed off rejections of *A Breaking and a Death*.

"You know I've always liked this book, and thought someone should take it," Volkening wrote on June 28, 1954, referring not to the volume of poems but to *Fall Quarter*. Yet the Keeses' household was hardly the environment for reconsidering the novel. The literary agent's solicitous letter arrived when Kees was being overwhelmed by Ann's drinking problem and the deterioration of their marriage. Within a week she would be institutionalized during the July 4th holiday. And their divorce followed two months later, handled by the same A.C.L.U. lawyer who had defended Tokyo Rose.

"It seems to me that the atmosphere is now such," Volkening continued in his letter, "[for] the satirically sad-gay novel that you would enjoy doing." Yet how surreal this idea must have been to Kees as he watched his wife drink.

The outward signs of Ann's breakdown, along with the reclusive life she led until her death in 1975, can never disclose what lay behind her close connection to her husband's career at its ebb, when he had strayed from writing poems that could not find a publisher to writing jazz lyrics that did not sell. But it must have contributed to her decline, a decline that anticipated Kees's own crisis a year later.

Like many of the wives of the writers and artists of this period, she forfeited a creative life of her own in order to support her spouse's. Ann held jobs to meet expenses so that her husband could devote time to writing and painting. Whenever the rejections piled up in the face of her belief in her husband's genius, they were just as much her setbacks as they were his. After *Fall Quarter* came back from Knopf, for example, it was Ann who said: "We'll see it published if we have to print it ourselves."

At the age of forty, Ann Kees may have succumbed to the crisis Kees was well aware of in the weeks before he disappeared in the summer of 1955. In an essay by Raymond Nelson, "The Fitful Life of Weldon Kees," one could read into the crisis of the writer the crisis of the writer's wife, the woman who patiently waits for her husband's success—but it does not come:

[Kees] talked to his father about Malcolm Cowley's

The Literary Situation, especially the passage describing the forty year crisis to which writers are liable: how disillusioning, how traumatizing it is to be forced to confront the passing of one's youth and promise, to acknowledge that one's future is likely to resemble his past. For artists, who are inclined to compare themselves to the great masters of their craft, it is often a time of nervous breakdowns, extreme dissipations, and other desperate remedies.

Volkening may have apprehended this turning point in Kees in the autumn of 1954, whose remaining months resembled the life of one of his characters, living in a few small rooms with his cat "Lonesome," affecting black sheets on his bed and taking up with a platinum blonde, Berkeley co-ed who made her living as a stripper. Or perhaps Volkening was just being a good businessman when he gently urged Kees to return to his active list of novelists, feeling it absurdly wasteful for a talented storyteller not to write fiction. In an attempt to coax *Fall Quarter* from its author, the literary agent reminded Kees of the aspirations he had left behind in the 40's, writing: "It will make you feel younger."

A NOTE ON THE TEXT

Two manuscripts for *Fall Quarter* exist. There is the one used by Kees's literary agent, Henry Volkening, now in the Berg Collection of the New York Public Library, and Kees's ribbon copy, in the Heritage Room of the Bennett Martin Public Library in Lincoln, Nebraska.

One difference between the two manuscripts worth special attention is the novel's beginning. There are additions to the text which register Kees's awareness of how the prewar world of *Fall Quarter* had been strangely made more remote by America's involvement in the Second World War, a remoteness that brings out the appealing madness of the novel's environment and dramatis personae. Kees did this by adding, in light pencil, to Volkening's copy: "All this happened a long time ago." Later he revised and expanded this opening in the Heritage Room copy. Like putting a modern facade on an old building, Kees hid the novel's prewar origin, disguising *Fall Quarter* as a postwar novel.

This edition of the novel is not very different from the version the Knopf editors read in 1941. It is based on the Heritage Room copy, which contains numerous holographic corrections. In preparing a final manuscript, I have also added salient corrections Kees did not harmonize from the Volkening manuscript. It is likely he did not have access to this copy when he worked on *Fall Quarter* for the last time. What became the final version of the novel probably occurred in the summer of 1954. A letter from Volkening, dated August 24, acknowledges Kees's decision to return to *Fall Quarter*: "As for the novel, Weldon, I'm glad to hear you plan reworking it. I'll do my best to place it." The revisions Kees made, however, were never conveyed.

ONE

On a fall afternoon, several years before he was to be drafted to fight in the Second World War, a young man named William Clay sat in the day coach of a train that traveled between Chicago and Kansas City. He watched the conductor going up the aisle to remove small pieces of pink cardboard from the metal clamps above the seats as sun-baked and desolate farmland gave way to a village, a general store with tin signs advertising flour, tobacco and female remedies, a bank with boarded-up windows, an unpainted church. Two dogs were fighting in the middle of the main street. The train whistle shrieked; once again he viewed the same flat land. William Clay took out his watch, a present from his uncle on his graduation from college. It was a few minutes after four o'clock.

He was a bright-looking young man of twenty-five. He wore a plain dark suit, a white shirt, and a small-patterned tie of white and blue. He had worn nothing but white shirts and small-patterned ties since he had been an undergraduate. On his watchchain was a gold key signifying membership in Phi Beta Kappa; this was his only piece of jewelry except for a pin which held the points of his collar in place. Even after the exhausting night on the train, sleeping in the chair car, he still looked sufficiently alert to step into a classroom and initiate freshmen into the mysteries of syntax.

Three months before, William Clay had distinguished himself by successfully completing his requirements for the Master of Arts degree in English Literature. This had been at a large university in the Middlewest. His professors had been unable, in spite of all their efforts, to trip him up in his orals. He had fallen down on only one question; he had been unable to furnish them with the date of Sir Thomas Wyatt's death. It was regrettable, but he knew it now: 1542. He was not likely to forget it again.

Besides the impression he had made while the five men fired questions at him, some of them zealously and some with an air of weariness, Dr. Gormley had praised his thesis on Richard Crashaw unreservedly. Dr. Gormley had been particularly impressed with William's discussion of vowel sounds in the poet's work. Indeed, Dr. Gormley had gone so far as to recommend that William's thesis be published by the University in its "Studies in Language and Literature" series. In going over the manuscript for publication, William had composed a preface which contained this sentence: "It is impossible to find words with which to indicate my deep gratitude to Julius Adelmo Gormley, whose careful reading of this study has saved me many an error."

The publication of the thesis, however, had been postponed for a short time, due to the rush of work at the University print shop; overdue were the Fall announcements, the season's first issue of the campus humor magazine, not to mention the monumental work of Dr. Blatter, of the Department of Biology, on wheat rust.

William Clay's academic successes had made it easy for him to find a position. His future seemed assured. He would teach freshman English for two years in the university of a nearby state, as his contract specified, saving as much money as he could for work in the East on his Ph.D. On completion of his doctorate, he planned to marry Frances Hyatt, a girl from his home town. These next two years of teaching, he hoped, would be full and productive. He planned to write several articles for the scholarly journals.

He was looking forward with enthusiasm to meeting his first class. While a sheet of ruled paper was passed around the room for the roll, he would speak of literature and language in a way calculated to arouse their interest; the work of the year would be explained; he might even tell a joke; he would bring up the matter of the text they would be required to purchase.

The train jolted and William Clay was distracted from thoughts of these pleasant prospects. A small crowd waited on the station platform and a few baggagemen were standing by hand trucks, looking dolefully at the train.

Taking his luggage from the rack, he wondered what his first move should be. A redcap took his bags and he got into a taxi. From a Chamber of Commerce bulletin for which he had sent, he had learned that a good medium-priced hotel was the Bryant.

"Bryant Hotel," he said.

"Yes, sir," said the taxi driver, an evil-looking man with a pockmarked face.

Although it was the tenth of September, it was still unbearably hot. Passing a mammoth thermometer on the side of a bank, with a tube of neon light indicating a temperature of 104 degrees, he wished for a moment that he had taken the job he had been offered in the Northwest. The town was old, run-down, and ugly; most of the buildings were constructed of an unusually dirty gray stone. Dust blew in the streets.

"When do you have autumn here?" he asked the taxi driver.

"How's that?"

"When does it begin to cool off?"

"You got me. We've had the heat record for the whole country now for the last five days."

William Clay leaned back in the seat, wondering suspiciously if the driver were not taking him to the hotel by some circuitous route, and wiped the

perspiration from his forehead with a white handkerchief that had the initial "C" embroidered in the
corner.

   His room looked out on the tops of buildings, covered with dust and dry leaves. There was a large
flat structure resembling a warehouse across the street.
It had "Dreamland" painted on one side.

   He unpacked his white linen suit and sent for a
bellboy to take it out to be cleaned, explaining to
him in detail the manner in which he wished the
lapels rolled. After he had bathed and shaved, he
moved about the room in his underwear, elated with
the excellence of the hotel's air-conditioning. The
Chamber of Commerce people had made no mis-
take in recommending the place. He unpacked his
bag, neatly arranging his belongings in the closet
and the dresser drawers, after rubbing his index fingers
inside them first to make sure that they had been
properly dusted. From the bottom of the bag he
took out an india-paper edition of *The Oxford Book
of English Verse.* He sat down and lit a cigarette,
which he smoked only half of the way down; he
had read a paper by a scientist who had pointed
out the deleterious effects of smoking more of a cigarette than this.

   He could not concentrate on Wordsworth. Perhaps he should call Dr. Showers and let him know

that he had arrived. Still, there was no rush; he was not expected until the next day. Dr. Showers might even be irritated by a call at this time. William was well acquainted with Dr. Shower's book on Swift, which he considered a work of considerable merit. He sat looking out at the dancehall.

After a while he dressed and rode down in the elevator and had a martini in the bar of the hotel. Two attractive and fashionably dressed women in their thirties, both of whom wore large, expensive engagement and wedding rings, were the only persons in the bar. They had reached the point at which laughter comes with much ease. One of them kept looking at William in interest.

Delicacy prompted him to refrain from eating the olive in the martini. When he left the bar, conscious of the women's eyes on his back, he walked erectly, his head held very straight. It was the least good-looking one who had been flirtatious. He rather wished it had been the other. He wondered if it could possibly be true—all these stories on marital infidelity that one heard.

He went out into the heat. A slight incline led to the residential district. He knew from his map of the city that the campus on the University was beyond that. The sun was beginning to go down. The drab houses, with tired men and women fanning themselves on the porches, depressed him, and the closer he came to the campus the more drab both the houses and the people became. He had rather counted on a more attractive city.

At a restaurant he ate cold meat, sliced tomatos that were too warm, and a peculiar-tasting potato salad. The coffee was not good. He walked on to the University.

The campus buildings were much alike, except for several of red brick, recent additions. The others were of the same variety of gray stone so much admired by the contractors of the city. As it grew dark, a faint breeze began to stir. He walked around the campus with a feeling of already belonging to it. Here he would hurry along on winter mornings to his eight o'clock classes. There would be persons who would call out, "Oh, hello there, Clay!" Since there were several notable scholars on the campus besides Dr. Showers, there was no reason why he might not soon be on speaking, if not intimate, terms with some of them.

He found the dark building in which he would teach. It was Needham Hall, one of the new additions. In the dim light he could make out a mural above the main door. It showed a rather heavy-set woman in a white gown who was apparently leading a number of persons, looking strangely stunted, from darkness into light.

Walking back to the hotel, he thought of the letter he would write to Frances Hyatt. He had been more or less engaged to her for several years, although there had been no formal commitments. He made a practice of writing to her once a week. She wrote oftener.

But he was lonely when he returned to the hotel, and the disturbing and plaintive melody that came from the jukebox in the bar drew him there again.

The bar was crowded. A number of fraternity boys, down for rush week, glanced at him as he came in. One of them was balancing a napkin holder on his forehead, and another was attempting to make a spoon jump into a glass. Still another was unscrewing the top of a pepper shaker. One large booth, filled with what William took to be representatives of the younger married set of the city, exuded an air of fashionable boredom.

> *You're my thrill.*
> *You do something to me,*
> *Send the chills right through me,*
> *When I look at you I can't sit still:*
> *You're my thrill.*

The jukebox alto sang this selection throatily; then there was a blare of brass; then clarinets and strings.

William Clay sat up to the bar and ordered a scotch and soda, turning to look at a couple who were coming in from the street entrance. It was the girl who claimed his whole attention. He could not take his eyes from her. Never before in his life had he seen anyone so desirable. Her heart-shaped face had a look of both innocence and sensuality; her dark hair was lustrous and worn in a long bob, and she had the most beautiful body, the finest small pointed breasts, that he ever hoped to see. Her eyes were gray, or perhaps green, and they slanted minutely. It was perfectly understandable that William Clay fell for her completely and at once.

"That'll be thirty-five," the bartender was saying.

William had a feeling, when the words sank in, that the man had said it several times. He hastily laid some change on the counter, and attempted to swallow some of the drink with an air of self-possession.

The girl sat down with her companion in the only empty booth. It was William's good fortune to be in such a position that, by turning slightly, he could watch her with ease. It was marvelous to William to watch her smooth her skirt as she sat down, the lowering of her eyelids as the blond man lighted her cigarette. He was entranced. He wanted to know her name. He wanted to know everything about her. For the man with her he had nothing but detestation. He seemed a surly individual, scarcely five feet four, and had a soiled and rumpled appearance. He was arguing with her. He would shake his head vigorously, his chin jutting forward; but the girl only smiled at him apparently amused. She looked about nineteen. Even in the plain green dress, with no jewelry but tiny earrings, she seemed to belong anywhere but in this Middlewestern hotel bar. He mentally undressed her, then put her clothes on again and repeated the undressing. Her beer, he noticed, was untouched.

Someone was nudging him.

"You got a match, pal?" the man sitting next to him was saying.

He gave him his book of matches and waited while the man, who was rather drunk, struck three of them before he got his cigar going.

William attempted to turn away to look at the girl again, but the man laid his hand on his arm and said, "Say, did you hear the one about the plumber who was working in the bathroom and the kid who kept asking him questions all the time? That's a funny son-of-a-bitch. You heard it?"

"Yes."

The man was very persistent. "How about the one about the Indian who could never get all he wanted?" he asked, smiling broadly. "That's a dilly, that one."

William listened with half an ear. When the storyteller laughed to indicate the wow of the anecdote, William smiled vaguely and looked around for the couple.

They were gone. He left his drink unfinished and went out into the street. A taxi was just pulling away from the hotel, and through the window he

could see her as she threw away her cigarette. The
taxi gathered speed and turned the corner. He stood
for a long time on the sidewalk and then returned
to his room to write a letter to Frances on the hotel
stationary. It was a tedious undertaking. The stationary had a picture of William Cullen Bryant on
it. William wrote chiefly of the intense heat and how
much he missed her.

After undressing and putting on his pajamas, he
sat in the chair by the window, trying to read the
newspaper. It was not long before he switched off
the light and sat in the darkness, looking out at the
lights blinking over the town. Without realizing it,
he smoked three cigarettes in rapid succession, down
as far as they could be smoked.

T W O

The first two floors of Needham Hall were given
over exclusively to the Department of English. The
third floor was occupied by the College of Dentistry,
from whose classrooms came the sounds of drilling
and pounding, and the Department of Greek and
Latin Languages, now reduced to a rather pathetic
three faculty members. Many persons assumed that
there were four men in the Department of Greek

and Latin Languages because of the frequent presence in the building of Dr. Buckman, Professor Emeritus of Greek, an unpleasant old man with a dirty white beard, who, though he had been retired for some years, was unable to stay away from his former habitat. This greatly irritated his former colleagues, who objected strenuously to Dr. Buckman hovering about and nosing into things. It seemed to them that Dr. Buckman spent more time in the Department since his retirement than when he had been on the active list.

The building had been completed and in use for several years, but the composition floor still gave off an unappealing aroma which it had had from the beginning. Heads of departments and full professors protested bitterly about this smell from time to time to the University officials. It did no good. They were always informed soothingly that the smell would eventually go away and that, besides, the composition floor had been very costly. It had, as a matter of fact, been purchased from one of the trustees, who was doing very well in the contracting business.

Because of the atmosphere in Needham Hall, it had been christened "The Stable" by Mr. Grauch of the College of Dentistry. Mr. Grauch was something of a wit in the laboratory on the third floor. Another term, less euphemistic, was in use among some of the male student body and among faculty members with a Rabelaisian turn of mind.

Dr. Henry Blanchard Showers, the head of the English Department, had the largest office in the building. It was at one end of the second floor, where he had a fine view of the campus, particularly of Woodruff Hall, home of the Botany and Biology Departments. Now and then, when Dr. Showers looked up from his work to rest his eyes, he would see persons in white jackets dissecting something. This was distressing to Dr. Showers, who was a mild antivivisectionist.

Dr. Showers's office was a stronghold of disorder. His desk, at one end of the room, was one of the largest rolltop models ever built, and it made the professor appear to be much smaller than he was. It was littered, too, on top, on the work space, and on the little shelves that slid out on either side and which were never pushed in, with countless papers, books, magazines, paperweights, pens, pencils, notebooks, and other odds and ends. These flowed over on to a table next to the desk. Dr. Showers was in the habit of making notations of thoughts that came to him, or reminders of things to do, on almost anything he could get his hands on. These scraps of paper were everywhere. Dr. Showers was opposed to filing them, and it was astonishing how often he was able to put his hands on just the paper he wanted. It was, in some ways, his most noteworthy accomplishment.

On one wall was a large green and purple hanging which had been presented to Dr. Showers by a friend of his who now taught at the University of Oklahoma. His friend had brought it from the Orient. It had some symbolic meaning which Dr. Showers's friend had not been able to recall at the time of the presentation. It hung in Dr. Showers's office because the professor's wife would not have it in their home. Mrs. Showers was a woman of some taste. It had been hanging in one place or another, wherever Dr. Showers's office happened to be, for many years, and had faded a good deal, causing him to revise his opinion of the genius of Orientals with dyes.

Also in the room were a bust of Swift, one of Matthew Arnold (another gift), and a reproduction of the Winged Victory, which Dr. Showers had picked up for a pittance at a junk shop. All three were fly-specked; and the bust of Swift, which had been lugged around from place to place a good deal, was cracked at the base. There was a clock, out of the 'nineties, which had not run since the Harding administration, its hands stopped at two-fifteen. On the wall were framed diplomas, showing Dr. Showers's degrees. There were two bookcases, one for sample textbooks presented by publishers, and the other for books that Dr. Showers had read or intended to read sometime. Another shelf held volumes he had neglected to return to the library.

While waiting for William Clay to arrive for his appointment, Dr. Showers was working on a few things he had to get out of the way before morning, one of which was a speech he was going to make at faculty meeting the next day. His eyes were beady with concentration as he worked on the notes for it.

Some men rise to positions of importance or power through chicanery and craftiness; some through relatives or friends; some through the possession of the exact amount of mediocrity required by their superiors; some by so great a superiority that enormous difficulties are presented to those who wish to hold them back; some by circumstances alone; some by seniority and age. Dr. Showers owed his position as head of the Department of English to his age: he was the oldest member of the department when Dr. Thigpen's death created the vacancy. Dr. Thigpen, the former head and distinguished authority on the Victorian period, had been run over by an automobile operated by a middle-aged woman who was just learning to drive.

There had been a good deal of clandestine rejoicing when the news of Dr. Thigpen's demise got around. The old man had been known for years around the campus as an "interesting character." This reputation was due principally to his weirdly-trimmed white whiskers, his flowing ties, and the ivory-headed cane he carried. He was given to thrusting the cane at dogs he came upon. He disliked dogs intensely.

Once, when a dirty tan dog, starved and harmless, wandered into his office, Dr. Thigpen had been thrown into a fit of rage that had lasted for many days.

His eccentricities were smiled upon by the University as a whole; the clandestine rejoicing came from the members of his own department, who knew the Doctor for what he was. Few "interesting characters" can stand up for long at close quarters. In most cases they are soon discovered to be bores, fanatics, or basically uninteresting persons with a few surface traits or characteristics which are responsible for their apparent distinction. The men under Dr. Thigpen, fully aware of this truth, were not unhappy to see him go; and since there was but one obvious choice for his successor, any bitterness that existed over the appointment of Dr. Showers was inconsequential.

Dr. Showers resembled those men whose pictures are frequently seen in photographs of small-town Chambers of Commerce. They usually are to be found standing in the back row. Often the photographer, if he is a stickler for symmetry, finds a book or a box for them to stand on.

Dr. Showers was sixty-one, and looked much younger. He was a short, stout man, as neat in his personal appearance as he was disorderly in the care of his belongings. He wore dark blue suits with white pinstripes. He had four of them, not one of which could be distinguished from the others. He was bald and wore rimless glasses. Twice a week he played golf, and this was responsible for his good tan. He was the healthiest-looking member of the department, on the whole a rather pale and undernourished lot except for Mr. Calmer, who had very red cheeks and had played football as an undergraduate, up to the time he had ruptured himself.

Dr. Showers worked diligently, if not hard, and expected those beneath him to follow his example. His book on Swift was a testament to his diligence and thoroughness; it was one of those books in which the author has not only squeezed the lemon dry, but has also added generous portions of the rind.

The first detail William Clay noticed, upon coming into the corridors of Needham Hall, was the smell. He wondered if something had died in the place. The building was cool, however, although it was already very hot outside. William could not understand why it smelled so bad. He hoped it was a temporary condition.

He was anxious to meet Dr. Showers and talk things over with him. He was eager to get settled in his own office.

The only person he met on the way up to Dr. Showers's office was an old man sweeping the floors. He asked him if he were going in the right direction, and the man merely nodded.

In the few seconds that elapsed between William's knock and the opening of the door, William felt of the knot of his tie, glanced at his fingernails to make sure they were perfectly clean, and straightened his shoulders. He also arranged a smile on his face that he hoped was pleasant.

"Well, you are certainly prompt!" Dr. Showers said, extending his hand and grinning. He held the door open with his foot. "Come in and sit down."

Dr. Showers would have known William anywhere from the photographs he had received with William's letter of application and scholarship records. He was pleased that William lived up to the pictures. The people he hired often did not. Usually, when selecting a new man, Dr. Showers went directly to the source, to Chicago or Harvard or Yale; but this time he had been vacationing with his family in Los Angeles when he had had word that Mr. Burton was not returning. William's letters of recommendation had been so fine, even in a profession where such documents often contain numerous purple passages, that there had been no question of not hiring him.

Dr. Showers cleared a pile of books and papers from a chair and indicated that William was to sit on it.

"Too bad you had to come at a time like this," Dr. Showers said, offering William a cigarette. "This is the hottest September I can recall."

William rose to the occasion and lit Dr. Showers's cigarette for him, noticing that they were a brand he did not care for.

"It is hot," he said. "But I've been looking forward so much to this year that I haven't minded it much."

Dr. Showers nodded. "I don't mind it, really, either," he confided. "But my wife and daughter! They complain all the time. We no sooner got through with one vacation in California and got settled here again than they decided the heat was too much for them and went out to Estes Park. Colorado, you know."

"Yes," said William.

"The men you took your work under certainly said some mighty fine things about you, Mr. Clay. You're going to have a hard time living up to them."

"I don't doubt that, Dr. Showers."

"Dr. Kingston—how is he these days?"

"Oh, fine. He's getting pretty old, of course."

"Yes, yes, I suppose. And Dr. Gormley?"

William brightened at the mention of Dr. Gormley's name. "First-rate. I don't believe I wrote you that he's going to get my thesis published by the University."

"That's most encouraging; very glad to hear it. There's nothing like publishing, getting in the habit of publishing when you're young in the profession. So many young men don't realize the wisdom of that." Dr. Showers shook his head sadly at the thought of these unthinking young men.

There was a silence, during which they could hear the janitor banging his broom against the wall. William, catching sight of the bust of Matthew Arnold, gazed at it curiously. He had never before seen a bust of the author of *Culture and Anarchy*, and it interested him, even though he did not wholly approve of Arnold, for William's focus of interest was in the Seventeenth Century.

"Have you found a place to stay yet?" Dr. Showers asked.

"No, not yet. I'm staying at one of the hotels for the time being. I thought you might be able to suggest some place."

Dr. Showers rubbed his chin thoughtfully. "Well, if you wanted to be close to the campus, there are quite a few apartment houses in the neighborhood; but most people find it more pleasant to live on the other side of town, or closer to the business district. Do you have a car?"

"No."

"It's difficult if you don't have a car. Of course, too, maybe you don't want an apartment."

"Well, I'd thought a little of getting my own breakfasts."

Dr. Showers nodded as though to indicate that he thought this a very praiseworthy intention. After they had talked for some time about living quarters, they went on to politics, the state of the theatre, trends in teaching, and golf. The conversation on the subject of golf soon developed into a lengthy monologue by Dr. Showers, which was interrupted by the ringing of the telephone.

While he was talking to someone who seemed to be reminding him of an appointment, the door of the office opened to admit a very wizened little man. He carried a briefcase and was smoking, or rather holding in his mouth, a pipe of the sort affected by ex-Vice President Dawes.

Dr. Showers rang off and turned around in his swivel chair, brushing against some papers and knocking them on the floor.

"Well, Henry!" he exclaimed.

The two men shook hands and the newcomer was introduced to William as Dr. Wilkinson. He had a very strong grip and did not smile.

"Mr. Clay," Dr. Showers said, "is taking Mr. Burton's place."

"Hmmm," said Dr. Wilkinson.

"How was your trip, Henry?"

Dr. Wilkinson shrugged, took the pipe from his mouth, and looked around for some place to spit. He walked over to the window and opened it. He put his head out of the window and made a noise.

William was aware that not much had been settled, but felt he had stayed long enough and should go.

"Oh yes, Mr. Clay," said Dr. Showers. "There'll

be a meeting of the people in the department day after tomorrow at ten in the morning. Can you make that?"

"Certainly."

Dr. Wilkinson was wiping his mouth with the back of his hands. He picked up a magazine, one of the philological journals, and glanced through it with noticeable displeasure. His gray flannel suit was several sizes too large for him and his necktie was frayed. He wore, on his right hand, two large rings. He kept making noises in his throat as if attempting to clear it.

"I'm going to put you down on the first floor," Dr. Showers went on. "Your office will be number thirteen. Nothing unlucky about that, I hope." He laughed briefly to let William know that something amusing had been said.

Rummaging around under the debris on his desk for some time, he finally drew out a small cardboard box. From it he took a key. He examined it with care. "Yes, that's the one," he said, giving it to William.

Dr. Wilkinson was striking a match on the base of Matthew Arnold's bust.

"Well, day after tomorrow, then!" said Dr. Showers.

"Good-bye," William said. He wished them good morning and added that it had been a pleasure to have met them both. Dr. Showers smiled pleasantly, but Dr. Wilkinson did not even look up. He made a sound in his throat.

William went out into the bad smell of the hall. On the whole, it had been a rather disappointing meeting. Still, Dr. Showers seemed like a decent sort. He tried the key in the door of the office numbered thirteen. It did not fit. He put the key in his pocket and went back to the hotel.

THREE

William spent the afternoon, which was as hot as the one on which he had arrived, looking for living quarters. At one house, just before he arrived, the plaster had fallen off the ceiling in the living room. At another, a woman came to the door in her bare feet. They had not been bathed for some time. A girl sat in the front room, which was completely empty except for the chair on which she sat, playing *La Paloma* on a Hawaiian guitar. Their rooms smelled of formaldehyde. In one of them was a stuffed two-headed cat. There were several small apartments elsewhere that he liked, but they were a little expensive.

At four-thirty, when he had almost given up, he found just what he was looking for. It was a large room with six windows, a fireplace, and two closets, one of which was equipped with a small sink and gas plate. The woman who showed him the room was a tall, aristocratic-looking woman with prematurely white hair. She had a flat chest and her arms were very thin. A Pekinese with sore eyes wandered about the room after following them up the stairs.

William knew at once that he would take the room, but he looked it over carefully as a matter of course, pulling out the dresser drawers to make sure that they did not stick, feeling of the bed, speculating on how the light would be in the mornings.

"This room was just vacated yesterday," the woman said, snapping her fingers at the Pekinese, who was showing signs of wanting to jump on the bed. "The woman that had it lived with us for two years. Mrs. Medbury. She came from a very good family. Perhaps you know the Medburys here?"

"No," said William. "I moved here only the other day."

"They're a very fine old family here, but they had a lot of bad luck after Grandfather Medbury was poisoned," the woman said sadly. "Come here, Ming!"

The dog ignored her and the woman seemed to forget about it immediately. "The bathroom is down at the end of the hall. There are only two other people using it on this floor."

William completed his survey of the sink and the gas burners in the larger closet, satisfied that no gas escaped and that there was both hot and cold water. They went down to look at the bathroom. The Peke ran ahead of them and was chewing elatedly at a strand of toilet paper when they came in.

"I think you'd be comfortable here, very comfortable," the woman said. "It's quiet and we keep it hot in the winter. Of course, that's not a thing one wants to think about now."

They walked back to the room. William was especially taken by the neat carpet, very new, and the fresh wallpaper. He paid her a month in advance.

"May I move in this evening?"

"Certainly. I'll make out a receipt for you if you'll give me your name."

"William Clay."

"My name is Mrs. Esterling. I'll have everything ready for you by seven. I neglected to mention that the fireplace doesn't work." She called to the Pekinese and then looked at William sharply. "Where are you employed, Mr. Clay?"

"At the University."

"I see." It seemed to him that her expression changed slightly.

"I'm in the English Department."

"Oh, are you? My husband used to teach at the University."

She said nothing more until they had gone downstairs and she had given him a receipt for a month's rent.

"Good-bye, Mr. Clay," she said. "I'm glad you're

going to be with us."

She had a rather tragic manner, William thought. He wondered if Mr. Esterling were dead. Still, she had said "us." He went back to the hotel in high spirits at having found such pleasant quarters and called the express company to send his trunk around to the Esterlings.

After dinner he checked out of the hotel and took a taxi to his new residence. A tall, thin man with a black mustache was watering the lawn as he got out of the cab with his luggage. The man purposely avoided looking at him as he climbed the steps.

Mrs. Esterling met him at the door. "Everything's all ready for you," she said. "Just go on up."

On his way up the stairs, he heard her talking to the man who had been watering the lawn. William unpacked his bags and began the rearrangement of some of the articles in the room. He enjoyed the activity of getting settled. He thought he would sleep much better here. He had not slept at all well in the Hotel Bryant. The orchestra from the Dreamland dancehall played noisily and late. It seemed very quiet and peaceful here, however.

By the time he had unpacked his trunk, it was nine-thirty. He went downstairs. Mrs. Esterling was listening to the radio. The man with the mustache was sitting by the window. William asked her about storage space for his trunk.

"Oh, you can just leave it in your room for to-

night, if you don't mind," said Mrs. Esterling. "Hugh
will be glad to take it down in the basement in the
morning, won't you, dear?"

The man looked up. If, as his wife implied, he
welcomed such an opportunity, his expression did
not betray it. He had deep circles under his eyes
and appeared acutely weary and defeated.

"This is Mr. Clay, dear," said Mrs. Esterling. "Mr.
Clay, I'd like to have you meet my husband."

"How do you do," said William.

Mr. Esterling made no move to rise or to shake
William's hand; he merely looked at him with some
bitterness and then turned his eyes past him as though
William were no longer there.

"Your wife told me you used to teach at the
University," William said.

"Um."

"In what department were you?"

"Romance languages." Mr. Esterling gave William
a look that signified without any doubt that the
conversation, vexing and distasteful to him, was at
an end.

William stood uncertainly in the doorway. "Well,
good-night," he said. "I'm glad I met you Mr.
Esterling."

Mr. Esterling lit a cigarette.

"Goodnight, Mr. Clay," said Mrs. Esterling.

William returned to his room. What a boor Mr.
Esterling was! He certainly could say little for him.

No wonder, if he were in the habit of behaving so rudely, that he had been unable to hold his job. It was obvious that he had been fired. William would ask someone about him. Such rudeness was inexcusable. No doubt his wife had much to contend with.

He stood in the middle of the room, his mouth slightly ajar. His work concluded, he felt restless. Downstairs, someone seemed to be bouncing a golf ball. He paced about for a few moments, exhibiting all the signs of one who is endeavoring to come to some momentous decision.

Then, sitting down at the table, he wrote on a sheet of paper: "Things to do tomorrow. 1. See about phys. exam. 2. Get frame."

He contemplated these instructions for some time before he arose and went to the window. It was very dark outside. An airplane roared by overhead. From the house next door he could hear someone practicing, with more vigor than technique, the piano exercises of Czerny.

Remembering that he had not as yet completed the installation of his radio, he attached the ground wire to a pipe and switched it on. The light burned behind the dial, the radio hummed briefly, and a genial voice exclaimed, "Try Guthrie's Capsules for that bloated feeling!" William turned it off and went down to the bathroom.

The Pekinese was asleep in the tub. When he

removed the dog, it offered no resistance and stood, its pink tongue hanging out, watching William as he carefully cleaned out the tub before running bathwater.

"The assignment for tomorrow," said William, above the roar of the water in the tub, "will be the first thirty pages in the textbook. On Friday you are to hand in a theme, of not less than eight hundred words, on a topic suggested by your reading."

The dog barked sharply and ran down the hall. William felt of the water, burning his fingers.

"I would prefer," he went on, drying his hands on a towel, "that these papers be typewritten. Otherwise, they should be written on ruled paper, *on one side only.*" Smiling somewhat grimly, he returned to his room to undress.

FOUR

The doctor was a wiry little man who had a Southern accent and ancient false teeth with unappealing rose-colored gums. Completing his scrutiny of his watch, he returned it to his pocket, breathing heavily as he made notes of his discoveries on a chart.

"Open your shirt," he said in a gruff voice. William exposed his chest, hairless and rather undeveloped, to the cold touch of the stethoscope. The doctor listened with a dreamy expression while William studied the tufts of gray hair which, partially obscured by the hard rubber ends of the stethoscope, blossomed from the doctor's ears. He had found the doctor's name in the yellow pages of the telephone book.

The physician grunted noncommittally and jerked the ends of the stethoscope from his ears. He leaned back in his swivel chair and contemplated a stuffed eagle, frighteningly lifelike, that was mounted in a glass case on his desk.

"Have you ever used narcotics?" he asked.

"Never," William said.

"Hmm." The doctor scrawled some illegible marks on the chart, frowning as though the art of penmanship cost him some effort.

William buttoned his shirt and began to knot his tie. The office was dark and unpleasant; and he had not liked the look of a man waiting in the anteroom, who appeared to be suffering from the advance stages of some loathsome disease.

"You're in good shape," the doctor said. "Need more exercise, but nothing to worry about."

"How much do I owe you?"

"Three dollars."

William paid him and left the office with a resolve to exercise regularly. The man with the loathsome disease glanced up from an old copy of the

Elk's Magazine as William passed him and went down the stairs. Under an enormous white tooth, advertising a dentist who had offices in the same building, William stopped to light a cigarette before he set out to buy a frame for his Michelangelo reproduction.

It was reassuring to know that the doctor pronounced him to be in good shape, but he would have felt better had the doctor been a cleaner and more successful representative of his profession. A yearly checkup, however, always put William in better spirits.

The meeting was held in a classroom ordinarily used by Dr. Gunzel for opiating his classes on the Victorian poets. When William arrived, a few minutes early, after having successfully disposed of all his errands, several groups of people were animatedly talking. Alone in one corner was Dr. Wilkinson. He was apparently asleep. His mouth was open and his eyes were closed.

Several persons glanced at William. He felt ill at ease and did not know what to do with his hands. He looked for Dr. Showers, who soon entered the room carrying a briefcase. Greetings were called out; the members of the English faculty found seats; and a man who resembled the late William Howard Taft in his middle years awakened Dr. Wilkinson, who had begun to snore. Dr. Wilkinson opened his eyes and glared at the Taft man. "Catching a little sleep, eh, doctor?" the Taft man said in a manner no doubt intended to be jovial.

William found a place to sit in the rear of the room, but when the meeting began, Dr. Showers called to him, "Oh, Mr. Clay, come up a bit closer, will you please?" He stood up and took another seat next to a middle-aged woman who, in spite of the intense heat, was wearing a dark coat that was covered with what appeared to be dog hairs. "Are you Mr. Clay?" she whispered.

"Yes."

"I am Miss McVetchen. I hope we will see a lot of you. You must come over to my place for tea some afternoon. I'll introduce you to some of the most interesting people in town." Her eyes, inlaid in a circle of wrinkles, grew big; and William noticed with horror that her wrinkles were faintly colored with what seemed to be pink grease paint.

"That's very kind of you," he said, alarmed that his expression might have given evidence of his revulsion.

"Oh, you're going to like it here, I feel sure." Miss McVetchen went on to describe the many attractions of life in the town. Her hair was an odd color of gray-green, which William correctly guessed was the result of an unfortunate misreading of the directions on a bottle of dye. "But hush," she said, finally aware that quiet had fallen over the gathering. "Dr.

Showers is about to regale us."

As Dr. Showers got into his speech and the morning dragged on, William tried to determine why the
meeting had been called at all. Dr. Showers, warm-
ing to his subject, if it could be said that he had
one, dwelt at length on matters of the utmost banal-
ity, emphasizing academic details which could have
been far more significant, if at all, in a teachers' college
orientation course.

Many persons in the group took no pains to hide
expressions of acute boredom, while others wore smiles
that denoted complete accord, if not rapture, with
Dr. Showers's remarks.   When William suddenly
realized that he, too, was smiling horribly, he fixed
his eyes on the back of Dr. Wilkinson's head and allowed them to follow the little sprays of dandruff
that accompanied Dr. Wilkinson's scratchings. William discovered that he was paying no attention to
the speaker; he was thinking of the girl he had seen
in the Hotel Bryant bar. He was sitting in the bar
with her, and then they were going up in the elevator to a room that was far more luxurious than the
one he had occupied; he was locking the door; he
was beside her on the bed and, when he put his
hand under her dress, she had nothing on. She
wrapped her arms around him and gave him a kiss
that was long, passionate and maddening. He took
her dress off.

"So I would like to introduce Mr. William Clay, a

new member of the department," said Dr. Showers.

"That's you," Miss McVetchen whispered.

William stood up hurriedly and heard the sound of half-hearted applause. The meeting was soon over and Dr. Showers, radiant after the pleasure of conducting a meeting, introduced him to his colleagues. There was Miss Burnham, who had a very powerful handshake; Mr. Lund, a young man with warts on his face and an abundance of dirty, matted hair, who had an air of sulky thickheadedness; the William Howard Taft type, who giggled and was named Mr. Duncan; other persons named Mr. Calmer and Miss Burr and Dr. Fisher and Dr. Funk. There were still others whose names William did not catch.

"Don't forget to come over!" Miss McVetchen whispered loudly to William as the group began to break up.

He went down to his office and unlocked the door with a new key that Dr. Showers had given him. Sitting in a chair by the window was a man of about twenty-eight. He had a long jaw and a bristly red mustache and was wearing glasses which he took off as William opened the door and stood looking at him. He grinned at William and dropped ashes from his cigarette on the floor.

"How was the meeting?" he asked. "I thought I'd drop around to give you an unofficial welcome. The name is Devlin—Christopher Watrous Devlin."

"Oh yes," said William. "I think I saw it in the catalog."

"Splendid!" said Devlin, lighting another cigarette from the stub of the one he had been smoking. "It's in the catalog, all right. Mr. Devlin, Instructor. A.B., A.M. One year of maudlin behavior at various European universities." Devlin tossed the stub away. "That last part isn't in the catalog."

"Didn't you have to go to the meeting?"

Devlin registered astonishment. "Meeting! My dear Clay you astonish me! Any time I feel the need of that sort of thing I'll take it in a more primitive form. A hair shirt, an Iron Widow, or a movie with Don Ameche, yes. But one of those horrific little get-togethers, no. There are limits, after all. How did you come through the session?"

"It was pretty tiresome."

"I can imagine. And the learned scholars? Were you presented to them?"

William nodded.

"You'll grow to know and revere them," Devlin continued, taking a bottle from his pocket. "Take my word for it." He uncorked the bottle and extended it to William. "Have a bit of the life giver?"

"No, thanks."

"Just a little tonic my druggist fixes up for me," said Devlin, agitating the whiskey. "A simple formula compounded of healthful and nourishing ingredients. I find it the very thing for one after a difficult day. It has brought me many hours of solace." He took a long drink and made a face. "A bit heavy at this time of the morning, but one must overlook such things in the interests of hygiene. Wish you'd join me. I'm all over my trench mouth, if you need reassuring."

"How did you get in here?"

"My key fits several of the doors." Devlin took another drink. "It's rather convenient. I thought perhaps you might want a shot after the meeting. I remember with painful vividness the orientation I got two years ago when I was new here. It would have been worth a lot that day if someone had been around to wise me up." He gestured with his arm and put the bottle back in his pocket. "Oh God, I got up this morning with a fearful hangover and the best intentions in the world of going to the meeting. But I was late, and when I looked in and saw Showers going through his annual motions, I just couldn't bring myself to face it. I have days like this."

William sat down. "I'm a little disappointed in this place myself."

"It gets you," said Devlin. "You wouldn't believe it, but when I got this job I was the very picture of idealistic youth, with a burning desire to teach. Honestly! And look at me now. An old man in a dry month." He sighed. "Here I am up to my neck in debts, sick of this job, drinking too much, and the chances of them renewing my contract next year are unlikely, most unlikely."

"I can't make it out," William said. "I went up to see Dr. Showers and he didn't give me any infor-

mation about anything. Not a damned thing. I don't
know where I stand or when my classes are, or anything at all."

"Details, details," said Devlin. "A mere nothing,
my boy. That's the way it will be from now on in.
But I'll venture a prophecy. They'll give you two
or three classes in English 101g. It's all in the way
of seeing how much you can stand. If you can take
English 101g, you won't have any trouble."

"What's 101g?"

"101g," said Devlin, "is a class made up of freshmen who were dropped on their heads during their
formative years. There are others in the group who
were spared that experience, but who have names
that are disturbing. Vera Mae Jukes, Lowell Jukes,
Harold P. Kallikak, Norma Jean Kallikak. Students
who read with their lips moving and who experience great difficulty in spelling words of over five
letters. There'll be a lot of very tough young men
who will throw objects during the class hour. All
the girls chew gum. Oh, you'll like 101g."

"Did you have that class?"

"Did I have that class? Jesus, yes. Not only that,
but I also drew the freshman English course for
students of Dentistry. It's nice, too. Yes, I think
you can look forward to a happy year with us."

"Well, I guess I can stand it."

Devlin nodded. "I'm sure of it. A certain dead-
ening of the most rudimentary sensibilities is neces-

sary, and that takes time; but once you develop it, things go along swimmingly. And not only in 101g, but in the whole profession. A spirit of utter fatalism will turn the trick every time."

Outside, in the hall, the class bells, which were never disconnected, set up a ghastly ringing.

"Oh, fine," said Devlin.

William looked out the window. A man wearing dirty coveralls and a straw hat was pushing a machine which marked white lines on a tennis court. Across the street, several girls came out of a drugstore and waved gaily at a yellow roadster that was going around the corner at great speed.

"What drew you into this profession?" Devlin inquired.

William felt himself on the defensive. "Oh, I suppose it is pretty bad the first few years, but if a person does a good job of teaching and works hard, I can't think of anything more pleasant than teaching period courses in a good school."

Devlin raised his eyebrows and slid down in his chair, gravely examining the cuff of his trousers. "A pretty dream, Clay, a very pretty dream," he said. "What the hell, though. The things we do every day seem to be more and more the nervous jerkings of a dying chicken. Picture day after day of classrooms, the same badly-written papers on which you'll wear out your eyes in the small hours of the morning, the vacant faces of those who know nothing and want to know nothing. Perhaps the best thing we could do would be to teach moving-picture and radio-serial appreciation. It's a saddening business."

"Well, any job has its drawbacks."

"Too true," said Devlin. He dropped his cigarette on the floor and stepped on it. "Well, maybe you'll like it better than I have. I hope so. I suppose I'd better go up and see if I can explain my absence this morning to Showers."

"Why does it smell so bad in here?" William asked.

"It is rather high, isn't it?" Devlin sniffed delicately. "The floors are the offenders. But you'll get used to it, don't worry about that. You'll get used to it just as you'll get used to 101g."

He went to the door, where he stood for moment looking curiously at William and rubbing his hand over his chin. "Well, any time you need any help or advice, look me up. My office is down at the other end. I'll see you in a day or two." He paused and grinned. "Oh, by the way, did you meet Miss McVetchen and did she invite you to her salon?"

"I met her. What is it that she puts around her eyes?"

"God knows. Take my advice and go to see her. Once. Once only. It is quite enough. You might meet a freak or two."

"I doubt if I'll have the time."

"Oh, you'll find the time. Right now you're quite sure that your work will be fascinating as hell; but believe me truly, it won't be. Even Miss McVetchen's little gatherings will come as a relief. There's another woman here in town who considers herself the Mabel Dodge of the place, but she handles things on rather a different plane. I'll take you there sometime. She and Miss McVetchen, need I say, hate each other's guts." He raised an eyebrow and contemplated some distant object. "Well, so long." He hastily shook William's hand and went down the hall, the bottle bulging in his pocket.

F I V E

Devlin, it turned out, had been right. William was assigned to teach three classes of 101g. The students were very much as his colleague had described them: dull, stupid, or uninterested freshmen who sat during the class hour watching the clock, yawning, playing games with their pencils, staring out of the window, and exhibiting only the slightest concern for the fundamentals of language. A question such as: "What mark of punctuation is used to show the omission of a letter or letters from a word?" would fill them with embarrassment, and they would grow shifty-eyed, each hoping that he would not be the one on whom William would call. Unable to find anyone who knew what this mysterious mark of

punctuation might be, William informed them patiently that it was an "apostrophe," writing the word
on the blackboard. In the meantime, they would
look at him dully and count the minutes that had to
pass before the bell would ring and they could escape,
away from such tiresome and confusing activities.

He sat in his office, correcting a pile of themes
written by his fourth class, 101a, a brighter, but by
no means brilliant, group. It was Friday afternoon;
two weeks of school were over.

"I like to read, but I don't have much time," William
read, noting that the theme was written in green
ink on both sides of the paper, and that the student
had difficulty in writing on the ruled lines. "A 'too-
busy' life prevents me from doing as much reading
outside of school as I should like to do. Reading is
my delight and I like to do it all the time, even if it
is only the advertising in the buses. I like to read
the Epworth Herald, the Christian Advocate, Reader's
Digest, Vital Speeches, and other publications similar to these. As for novels, I have read many and
rank Harold Bell Wright as one of my best authors.
Why? Well, I suppose I like the way he can ana-
lyze mankind and also the beautiful pictures of the
scenes he paints."

William put a grade on it and laid it with the other
corrected papers. He wondered if his original
impulse—to assign a theme on "How I Spent My

Summer Vacation"—had not, after all, been a better idea.

He picked up another paper, apparently written in the back seat of an old car while traveling on a bumpy road. "I enjoy a good novel once in a while, can read political articles with a fair degree of intelligence, and appreciate Cooper and Kathleen Norris. I read Irwin Cobb and George McManus for the same purpose, but prefer Mr. Cobb."

William examined the endorsement. The author was Dorothy Mae Farquar. William recalled her as a hot little rock who sat in the front row with two of her sorority sisters and showed her legs, correctly surmising that such a display was unlikely to damage her scholastic record. He gave the paper a C-. Arranging the papers in a pile, he leaned back and lit a cigarette.

He had finished the papers in record time, even though he had been interrupted by a textbook salesman, noticeably intoxicated for that time of day, who had addressed William as "Mr. Burton," the name of the instructor whose place William had taken. William had got rid of him in short order.

That morning he had received two letters, and he took them from his pocket now to read again. One of them, from Frances, brought on an attack of loneliness and desire for her and he told himself that he would write her a good, long letter that evening. He would try to make plans for them to meet in Chicago at Christmastime. The other letter was from a friend of his who had been working on his Master's degree at the same time as William. He wrote to remind William of a girl he knew who lived in the town in which William was teaching. He had previously urged William to look her up. Her name was Janet Eliot. The address his friend supplied indicated that she lived in one of the wealthy residential districts.

It had been William's intention, when he took the teaching position, to have nothing to do with girls, a way of life he thought of as "being true" to Frances; but for over two weeks he had been working practically without rest on his classes, preparing lectures, correcting papers, holding conferences, and sleeping far too little. He felt that he now owed himself an evening of relaxation. There were only two Eliots in the telephone directory, and the address of C. D. Eliot corresponded to the one his friend Dockhorn had given him. He dialed the number and a man with a foreign accent answered. William asked for Janet Eliot. "A moment please," the voice said. A radio or a phonograph near the telephone at the Eliot's was playing Brahms. Evidently a family of culture, thought William.

"Hello," a girl's voice said sharply.

"Miss Eliot, Miss Janet Eliot?" he inquired.

"Oh, Herbert, for God's sake! I told you not to call me any more!"

"This isn't Herbert, this is William Clay."

She seemed to be choking. She finally seemed to

regain control of herself and said, "Who? Oh, Tod
Dockhorn's friend. What are you doing tonight?"

"I was just going to ask you the same question."

"Come out this evening. No, wait. Come out for
dinner. Say seven. Can you make it?"

"I'd like to very much."

"Seven o'clock, then."

William, replacing the receiver on the hook, raised
his eyes to see Devlin standing in the doorway. He
wore a roguish expression. "Well, well," he said.,
"I've heard everything. Janet Eliot. Just offhand I
would say that you were doing very well indeed.
If pressed, I'd go even further."

William was annoyed. He managed to smile
unconvincingly and say, "All right, consider yourself pressed."

"Ah, Janet Eliot!" Devlin said, taking a chair. "I'd
much rather spend an evening with her than T.S. or
George or the editor of the Five-Foot Shelf. Have
you ever seen the young lady?"

"No, I've never laid eyes on her."

"Very nice indeed," said Devlin, rolling his eyes
and moulding curves in the air with his hands. He
threw back his head and, out of the side of his mouth,
holding the cigar in the other corner, recited:

> "Her hair like gold did glister,
> Each eye was like a star,
> She did surpass her sister,
> Which pass'd all others far."

"Who's that?" Devlin said, giving William a penetrating look.

"George Wither."

"Born?"

"1588."

"Died?"

"1667."

"Splendid. Go to the head of the class."

"Does Janet Eliot have a sister?"

"Not that I know of. But she's got a lot of bright gold hair. I think you'll have a pleasant evening. Too bad, in a way, too. I came in to invite you to accompany me on a bust."

"Say, I'm sorry."

Devlin raised one hand in the manner of a preacher describing the quieting of angry waters. "There'll be other times." He picked up a theme from William's desk and allowed a strange look to appear in his eyes. "Well, well, listen to this . . . 'What books have I read lately? Well, now that you ask, teacher, I've been going over the hotter parts of the Decameron, Lady Chatterly, and Molly Bloom's coda in *Ulysses*. Pretty interesting stuff. Proust's fairies have intrigued me, and a Restoration comedy ain't bad. Have you ever read Pierre Louys?"

"Give me that!"

Devlin handed it to him. It was a theme by one Alvin Graub, who wrote that he read nothing but *Popular Mechanics* and the *Scientific American* and wanted to learn to be the pilot of a dive-bomber.

There were a great many red pencil marks on it, William's corrections.

Devlin had sunk down in his chair and appeared suddenly depressed. He gazed mournfully at his cigar and heaved a long sigh.

"What's the matter?" William asked. Devlin had gone up in his estimation considerably because of his ability to recall four lines of the obscure Wither.

"I'm in the dog house," Devlin said. "The other night I came out of one of the hotels, quite drunk, I'm ashamed to say, and bumped into Melvin Cathcart Lund. You know Melvin Cathcart Lund, don't you?"

"The Harvard one with the warts?"

"That's the one. Our specialist in recent prose literature. I don't know whether or not you're aware of it, but Melvin Cathcart Lund is a terrible toady and sycophant and has an ugly habit of running to Showers about every damned thing he sees." Devlin, noticing that his cigar had gone out, stuffed it in his trouser pocket. "I was pretty plastered, and I tried to get away from Melvin, but he tried to get me into a conversation, probably to find out just how tight I was. I'm afraid I said some things I shouldn't have." Devlin sighed again. "Showers knows I drink; there's more than one drunk in this department; the faculty of the University is literally lousy with dipsomaniacs. Unfortunately, I've done too many things around here that I shouldn't have. Sins of both omission and commission, I'm afraid.

I've been on the carpet a number of times, you know. It isn't that the old boy hasn't warned me sufficiently. I go up to his office and sit next to Matthew Arnold's bust—sort of comforting—and take my medicine like a little man. It's this unpardonable habit of mine of not meeting my eight o'clock frequently enough; that's bad."

"You really ought—" William began.

"I know, I know; I ought to meet them, agreed. I ought not to get fried in hotel bars, either. Well, I'll have to settle down one of these days, turn over a new leaf. I'm nearly positive that I won't get a contract for next year. And when Lund has finished telling Showers about my dreadful behavior the other night—well, I had better be thinking of looking for a position at Kansas Wesleyan or Nevada State Teachers College."

For a moment Devlin was a picture of despair; then suddenly he brightened and took a letter from his pocket. "Did you get one of these?" he asked. "Some guy at the School of Education is sending them out. He's doing a thesis on 'Faculty Opinion on the Meaning of Education.' He wants me to write at least five hundred words on what an education should do for one. Seems he's polling thousands of teachers all over the country."

"I didn't get one," William said, feeling rather left out. "What are you going to write for him?"

"Just one simple sentence, one simple little sentence. 'Education should prepare one for the Problems of Life.' Do you like that?"

"You really ought to take it more seriously," William said.

"Do you think so?"

"Yes."

Devlin selected a theme from the stack on William's desk. "'I like to read good clean outdoor stories like B. M. Bower's,'" he read. "What are you going to do about that?"

"There's no reason why that student won't be reading Chaucer with pleasure and understanding in a few years," William said.

Devlin stood up. "You going to stick around for a while?"

"Perhaps."

"I may be back."

When Devlin had gone, William went to the window to air out the room. It stunk of Devlin's cigar. He felt strangely depressed and unhappy. Like most persons of ambition and single-mindedness, he could not bring himself to accept what he knew was true: his classes had begun to bore him and then left him irritable and angry; there was no pleasure in wearily correcting the dreadful themes; his colleagues—with the sole exception of Devlin—ignored him; the amount of work he gave to the preparation for his classes was unappreciated; his students either disliked him or were indifferent to him; the building in which he worked gave off an odor that could only be described as dreadful.

Returning to his desk, he swept the themes into a drawer, lit a cigarette, and allowed himself to fall into a state of gloom mixed with the scant pleasure of feeling superior to his environment.

Dr. Showers could have given him better classes. It was absurd that a person with his gifts had to be wasted on such students as those in 101g. Melvin Cathcart Lund couldn't be more than a few years older than he was, yet had taught no freshman courses. Melvin Cathcart Lund taught only courses in his field of specialization. William thought it was certainly a fine thing when they couldn't let him give a course on the metaphysical poets. Devlin was right in many ways. College education for the masses was idiocy. A strong wave of antidemocratic feeling swept over him. If the worst happened, he might be stuck for the rest of his life teaching morons in some miserable State university.

His door was open, and a woman's voice from the hall floated in. "It's a lovely way to fix a cantaloupe. You can stuff them with crabmeat or pecans or anything you happen to have around."

"I must try it," another voice said.

He reached for a magazine and found the place at which he stopped reading.

"His dictum is inconsistent with the usage in Old English and in the Indo-Germanic language in general. In Old English verbs of Giving regularly took a dative of the indirect object and an accusative of the direct object, a fact attested by the form of the pronouns (*him*, dative singular, and *hine*, accusative singular) and of the definite article (*thæm* and *thære*, dative singular, and *thone*, *tha*, *thæt*, accusative singular). We know that with verbs of Giving the same differentiation between the dative of the indirect object and the accusative of the direct object was made in Greek and in Latin in both function and form."

When Devlin returned, William was still sitting at his desk. The magazine had fallen to the floor. "When are you going to Janet Eliot's?" Devlin asked.

"Seven."

"Dinner?"

William nodded.

"What's the matter? Could you use a drink?"

"Why not?"

"Follow me," Devlin said.

SIX

They walked across the campus to a section marked by a sign, "This Space Reserved for Faculty Parking." A young couple were necking in the back seat of Devlin's car, and the two instructors watched them with interest for a while. Finally, since their activity showed no signs of abating, Devlin went to the window and tapped with his finger.

The couple looked up with embarrassment. The girl hurriedly rearranged her dress. The young man wore a red sweater with "Dine and Dance at The Golden Lance" embroidered in yellow script on it.

"I shall have to speak to the Dean," Devlin said. He examined the back seat with care before opening the front door and inviting William to get in. Once inside, Devlin found an old pair of suede gloves on the floor and put them on.

They drove through a disreputable section of the city that William had not previously seen. When Devlin had to stop for traffic lights, he frowned impatiently, racing his motor. They crossed a bridge spanning a creek filled with stagnant water, rattled over railroad tracks, and finally drew up in front of an old house between a junkyard and a cluster of billboards. A sign on the door announced that this was the residence of Mrs. Gunnison, Chiropractor.

"An unusual point of interest in the city, and less public than the downtown bars," Devlin remarked. It was a wooden frame building of three stories, painted brown and decorated with wooden scrollwork and various cast-iron embellishments. The shades were drawn at the windows. They waited. Leaves were falling from the trees and a cold wind had come up. The season of the year impressed William with the impermanence of man.

A colored maid appeared in answer to Devlin's knock. She looked out cautiously and then smiled broadly at Devlin.

They went down a long bare hall, dark and smelling of dust, opened another door and seated themselves at a table with a red-and-white checked tablecloth. William looked at the paintings of nudes on the walls.

An enormously fat woman was approaching them.

"Well, Mr. Jones!" she said, addressing herself to Devlin. "It's been a long time."

"How are you, Mrs. Gunnison?"

It was impossible to tell where her bosom stopped and her stomach began. She smelled like a Woolworth cosmetic counter. There were deep circles under her eyes and she wore her hair long, done up in three large rolls, one on each side of her head and one in back. She wore three strings of beads and large pearl earrings.

"This is my cousin, Mr. Smith," Devlin said, introducing William. "Mrs. Gunnison."

"Delighted, Mr. Smith," said Mrs. Gunnison. "What will it be, gentlemen?"

They ordered scotch and sodas.

"Would you like to go upstairs and have a chiropractic treatment, Mr. Jones?" she asked solicitously.

"Not today, thank you," said Devlin.

"How about you, Mr. Smith?" She smiled widely, revealing a mouth full of gold.

William declined with embarrassment.

"I have several new practitioners who are very skillful," she said.

"Not today, Mrs. Gunnison," Devlin said. "Just bring us the drinks."

"Well, don't forget us any time it's anything in the chiropractic line," said Mrs. Gunnison to William with a fat smile.

She carried herself, in spite of her bulk, with much dignity. They listened to her going into another part of the house. Their drinks came and Devlin paid for them. The sounds of giggling female voices drifted down from the rooms overhead.

"Tell me more about Janet Eliot," William said.

Devlin sampled his drink, raised one eyebrow, and leaned back in his chair. He frowned slightly and passed his hand histrionically over his forehead. Any student of Devlin's would have recognized all this instantly—except for the movements connected with the drinking—as an integral part of Devlin's classroom manner.

Devlin said, "Janet's grandfather was a minor robber baron, old Tyler Eliot. I think you will find the old gentleman's name listed in the indexes of all the muckraking histories of American capitalism . . . Indexes? Do you prefer 'indices'?"

"Yes," said William. "I do."

"I prefer 'indexes,'" said Devlin. "It is given preference in the American dictionaries."

"But not in the English ones."

"Perhaps."

A weedy blonde in a velvet evening gown that was too tight for her came into the room and sat at the piano. She took off her rings, looking over at the table. "Oh hello, Mr. Jones!" she said to Devlin.

Devlin bowed very low. "Lois," he said.

"I had a card from Viola the other day," she said.

"How are things with her?"

"Never better," said Lois, who had begun to play the *Indian Love Call* on the piano, allowing her head to sway from side to side.

"An interesting case, Viola," said Devlin, finishing his drink and pounding on the table for another. The bartender came over and took away their glasses, after waiting for William to swallow the rest of his drink. "Viola was a very attractive girl who was in Mrs. Gunnison's services here for a while. She went out to Hollywood and in no time at all was playing ingenue roles in cowboy movies. Took us more or less by surprise. She works with somebody or other and his horse; White Lightning, I think the horse is called. Do you know the actor I mean?"

"No."

"I went to one of her pictures and it was all very lifelike. Somewhat more subdued, however, if you follow me." Devlin leaned his arms on the table and stared at his reflection in the mirror back of the bar. "Janet Eliot's mother and father are divorced.

She lives with her father who goes in for first editions and philanthropy and is said to take dope. Don't
suppose there's anything to it. Janet, as I've implied, is decidedly attractive. I envy you your
engagement with her. Her morals are alleged to be
rather lax. There may be nothing to that, either;
you know how eager people are to sully the reputation of an innocent girl."

The bartender brought their drinks. "Let me get
these," said William. He paid for them and then
sat for a moment turning the glass in his hand. "What
a relief this is after those classes."

"What you had to say about 101g was absolutely
correct."

Devlin nodded. "A stark bunch."

Lois concluded her rendition of *Indian Love Call*
with a lengthy glissando.

"They have a good dinge pianist in the evening,"
said Devlin.

William, who wished to bring the conversation back
to shoptalk, said, "Do you suppose there's any chance
of getting out of teaching 101g next year?"

Devlin shrugged his shoulders and watched Lois
put on her rings and glide from the room. The
bartender yawned and turned the page of the newspaper he was reading.

"Because if there isn't," William continued, "I'm
going to look for a job someplace else."

"101g must be regarded as a trial by fire," said

Devlin. "Turn yourself into a good Calvinist and you'll regard the whole business in a different light."

"I don't think I'd find that easy."

"Ah well," said Devlin. "It is Friday evening. You must get in the habit of never thinking about school over the weekend. That way lies madness."

"I suppose."

"101g is a necessary evil, it would seem, like Mrs. Gunnison's establishment. That reminds me, I had a girl in one of my classes last year who was working her way through school by holding a job here."

"You mean . . ."

"Yes."

"Astonishing."

"Quite a good student. I often wished she had drawn upon her vocation for theme material."

William glanced at his watch. "I guess we'd better go. I have to bathe and dress."

"By the way, where are you living?"

William told him.

"The name seems remotely familiar."

"Mr. Esterling said he used to teach at the University."

"Of course. The man who bounced a golf ball on the floor during his classes. I remember hearing about it now. Taught Portuguese, I believe. They had to get rid of him."

"Why?"

"Chiefly because of the golf-ball bouncing."

"I see."

"Did it constantly, I understand."

"Well, I must go."

"I'll buy another round," Devlin said.

"No, thanks."

They finished their drinks. Mrs. Gunnison appeared and invited them to return soon.

"Is the nature of this place well known?" William asked in a low voice as they prepared to go.

"More or less," Devlin said. "It used to be the only good bar in town during the 'twenties. They have a good cook here, a White Russian. Lots of people come here to eat who don't take advantage of the other, uh, commodities offered. As I said, it's less public than downtown. The whole setup gives people the illusion of being back in the prohibition era, only the liquor is cheaper and better."

They went through the hall. The colored maid was holding the front door open for a couple. William and Devlin passed them quickly, averting their eyes to some extent. William glanced at the girl. It was the same girl he had seen in the Hotel Bryant bar on his first night in town. She was prettier than ever.

When they were outside, William said excitedly, "Did you see that girl?"

"Yes."

"Who is she?"

"What's more important is this: Did you see the man?"

"I didn't get a good look at him."

Devlin opened the door of the car. "It was Melvin Cathcart Lund," he said.

S E V E N

The cab, with its meter ticking hysterically as though it were about to break, turned off the thoroughfare and passed through a grove of trees, emerging into a hilly district where, it was apparent, persons in the upper income brackets passed their days. It was dusk. William, in the back seat, gazed out at the widely separated houses, their windows yellow with light. A sunset that for some minutes had futilely been trying to come off, but had only succeeded in appearing rather murky, began to fade.

The taxi drew up in front of a large stone house and William got out and paid the driver. Before the iron gates that broke a gray stone wall around the Eliot estate, he paused a moment. In the middle of the sidewalk stood an extremely vicious-looking police dog with sharp brass spikes on its collar. It watched William quietly.

The cab was pulling away. There was no way out of it. The police dog, it seemed probable, would remain a good long time. William took a few steps and hesitated again as a low growl came from the animal's throat. Closer to him now, William could see that the dog was indeed an unlikable creature. One of its eyes was a normal color, while the other was a milky blue that added to its sinister appearance.

"Nice dog," said William.

At this, the dog barked suddenly and backed away, showing its fangs, its legs tense.

"God damn it," said William under his breath. He glanced around to see where he might run if the dog attacked him. He took several more steps, and again the dog barked and showed its teeth. It was just at this moment, luckily, that a man dressed in overalls came running around the corner of the house.

"Ranger!" he shouted, brandishing a heavy club. "Down! Down!"

He ran up to the dog and hit him several times with the weapon. The dog sank to the ground and began to whimper. The man smiled, showing teeth as yellow as the dog's; it was evident that he got a good deal of enjoyment out of letting the dog have a couple of good cracks with the club. "Vicious son-of-a-bitch," he observed genially to William, who had by now, as though again to prove the theories of John B. Watson, broken out in a cold sweat. He still eyed the dog with trepidation.

"Ah, you got to be tough with *that* son-of-a-bitch," the man said, taking the dog by the collar and giving him a jerk. "Of course, you were lucky; he wouldn't attack *you*. You got a dark blue tie on."

"What's that got to do with it?" William said.

"Ranger don't never attack people with dark blue ties," the man said. William thought him a lunatic. "It's a funny thing, but that's the way he is. If you'd been wearing any other color tie, it would have been a couple of big chunks out of you. Yes, sir."

William frowned. "A conditioned reflex of some kind, perhaps," he said doubtfully.

"You know best about that," the man said, dragging the dog around in back of the house and mumbling something to it.

William, considerably shaken, went up to the door and rang the bell. From inside the house he could hear sounds of a dance orchestra and, succumbing to curiosity, he peered inside and saw a young man standing in front of the phonograph. He was shaking animatedly and waving a baton, simulating the motions of a bandleader. As William rang again, he turned his head and, frowning, put down the baton and resignedly came to the door.

The blast of the phonograph was deafening. The young man stood looking at William.

"Yes?" he said. "What is it?"

William had to raise his voice to be heard, explaining that he had been asked there by Miss Janet Eliot.

"Oh, you came to see Janet, did you?" the young man said. He looked William over. "Well, she isn't here."

William hesitated.

"I suppose you want to come in and wait."

"Perhaps I'd better."

"I suppose you had."

He followed the young man into a huge room with many windows. There was a grand piano and on the floor a bearskin rug, over which William nearly tripped. He had not thought it possible that a phonograph could be played so loudly. Someone on the record was playing a trumpet.

"That's Bobby Hackett!" the young man shouted in William's ear.

"Oh."

"I like it good and loud," he explained. He was about twenty-one, very blond, with an alert, happy expression. The record came to an end and the phonograph stopped itself.

"You're not Jack Anthony, are you?" the young man asked.

"No."

"I thought you might be him, maybe."

"No."

"My sister's supposed to be engaged to a guy named Jack Anthony."

"Your sister Janet?"

"Sure. Who did you think? My other sister just got her divorce last month."

"Your sister's engaged to someone you've never seen?"

"I don't take much interest in it. What's you name?"

"William Clay."

"I'm Elliot Eliot. Hell of a name, isn't it?"

"Did your sister say when she'd be back?" William asked.

"Not to me."

"She asked me here for dinner."

"That's a good one," said Elliot Eliot. "The cook quit this morning."

William looked about the room. "Do you mind if I sit down?" he asked.

"You may as well. Do you like hot music?" Elliot Eliot did not wait for William to reply, although he had opened his mouth slightly as though something were forthcoming. Elliot Eliot took it immediately for granted that all persons except very elderly ones were hot music enthusiasts. Beaming happily, he selected a record. "You'll love this," he said. "Muggsy Alexander playing *Dead Man's Stomp.*"

This, then, was the life of the idle rich, William reflected, looking at a photograph on the piano. The photograph was of an extremely good-looking blonde girl. He leaned back in the chair and studied it with much interest, *Dead Man's Stomp* beating hellishly on his eardrums. Elliot Eliot, now completely captivated by the music and ignoring William, had begun to sway and stomp before the victrola, moaning hoarsely and waving one hand in the air.

William had eaten sparingly that noon. Always, when his appetite was unappeased for a consider-

able length of time, he became petulant and unhappy.
He now felt this way to a marked degree, for the
records, which Elliot Eliot played one after another
with undiminished zeal, were also having their effect.

William would have been pleased to know that
an opinion of great popularity among the Eliots'
neighbors was that a signal service would have been
performed by anyone boiling Elliot Eliot in oil.
Unaware of this, he suffered Elliot in silence, wondering if Janet would put in an appearance before
long.

He did not know how many records had been played
when, above the blare of the music, he heard a shriek
of brakes from the driveway. Shortly afterwards,
someone came up the steps and entered the house.

It was the girl whose photograph he had seen.
She was beautifully dressed and would have been
beautiful herself had it not been for the exasperated
expression she then wore.

"Elliot, turn that thing off!" she commanded. Then
she saw William. "Oh, you're Mr. Clay, aren't you?
My God, I'd completely forgotten about you. You
must be starved. Elliot, stop jiggling and please go
away or something." She said to William, "It's been
the most ghastly day I've known in simply ages.
Do you want to come with me? I've got to meet a
train."

William had several times begun to say something,

but there had been no opportunity. He watched her go into the hall. She was gone only a short time. She smiled briefly at him on her return, and they went out to her car, a long black roadster.

"You drive," she said.

In the front seat she stretched languorously and looked over at William as though for the first time actually seeing him.

"My God," she said. "The cook's quit and my father got in some mess or other and I've got to leave for Florida tomorrow and we've had the most upsetting news from my sister. And now I have to meet this train. You have no idea what a day it's been. Reach in the pocket there and you'll find a bottle. You just turn that key and the car starts."

It was a thermos bottle.

"Martinis," she said. "Have some."

She took a couple of drinks and handed the bottle to him. He slowed down and drank, feeling agreeably corrupt and shuddering perceptibly.

"Good, isn't it?" she said.

"Excellent."

"You know where the station is?"

"Yes."

"Can't you drive faster?" she said. "I scarcely feel I'm moving when I'm going less than sixty."

"I don't want to smash us up."

"Oh, don't worry about that! I've been in hundreds of accidents and never got scratched. Once I was with a boy and we ran right into a train and I wasn't hurt a bit."

"What happened to him?"

"He died."

William eased up a bit on the footfeed.

"Another time I drove right through a billboard. It's very easy to do. It was the funniest sensation. I remember it advertised some kind of peanut butter. I have wonderful luck that way." She drank from the thermos bottle and lit a cigarette. "Very refreshing, isn't it? Want me to light a cigarette for you?"

"Please."

She put one in his mouth. The end was red with lipstick.

"What is it you teach?"

"English."

"Is it any fun?"

"Fun? No, not exactly."

"I wouldn't think it would be." She pulled an ashtray out of the dashboard. "Are you a Communist?" she asked.

"No, of course not."

"I was with a boy one night who taught at some school in California. *He* was a Communist."

"Where did you go to school?"

"I went here a year, but it wasn't any fun. You know. I was in a sorority, a pledge, and they wouldn't let me do anything. I guess they thought I was a bad girl."

"Are you?" said William.

"Yes. Here's the station. My God, I wonder if that train is in already." She got out of the car. "You wait here and I'll see what's doing."

While she was gone, William helped himself to the martinis. A half hour passed. He got out of the car and went out on the platform. There was no train and no sign of Janet Eliot. He investigated the station. He had never been so hungry in his life and he put a nickel in a machine with a mirror and a chocolate bar came out of a slot. He went out on the platform again, munching on the chocolate bar, and was told by a man in overalls that the last train had come in twenty-five minutes before and left immediately.

He walked back to the car. It was no longer there. A filthy little boy was sitting on a monument near the driveway, apparently dismembering some kind of small animal.

"Did you see a car here?" William asked. "A large black car?"

"Some dame and a guy just drove away in it."

It was a long walk back to the business section. He went into the best restaurant of which he knew and ordered a huge meal. The effect of the martinis was beginning to wear off and he had a double brandy after dinner. It was enough to make one a revolutionary. He thought of all the insults he had endured in the past.

After a while he went out to the street. He could not bear the thought of going back to the Esterlings. He took a cab and gave the driver Devlin's address. Devlin was not at home. It was while they were driving back to town that he saw Melvin Cathcart Lund go by in his car. The girl was with him.

"You see that car?" William said.

"Yeh."

"Follow it."

They turned up a side street and for a time he thought he had lost them. Then he saw the taillight ahead.

"They're stopping up there," the driver said. "You want me to go on?"

"Pull up here," William said.

He stepped out in the darkness and paid the driver. The taxi drove away. Melvin Cathcart Lund's car was parked at the corner, and by the streetlamp William could see that he was examining the condition of one of the rear tires. William waited behind a tree. Lund kicked the tire several times and then got back in the car and drove off.

This was turning out to be a fine wild goose chase, William reflected. He counted his money. Four blocks away was a tavern. He walked back to it.

It was a green-and-cream place, narrow and poorly lighted. Along one side was the bar, with a long mirror behind it, and a sign: *If Father Is Going to the Dogs, Send Him in Here.* A man with a cigarette in his mouth was playing a battered piano.

William climbed on a stool next to a dumpy middle-aged woman. She sat with the dull, jolted look worn by some persons when riding in automobiles. Next to her was a nearsighted man with a green bow tie who looked down aimlessly at an empty shotglass before him. In one corner of the room stood a case enclosed in glass in which a miniature crane, operated by a fat, red-faced man, clawed ineffectually at articles resting in a bed of white beads.

"Double brandy," William said to the bartender.

The woman turned to look at him. She had on a great deal of makeup and was becoming slightly jowly. She was wearing a fur piece and a small black hat with an ornament on it that resembled a paper clip. Two strings of beads, red and black, swung from her neck. There were fine hair-like lines around her mouth and eyes, and longer ones that began at the sides of her nose and ran down her cheeks, disappearing into the recesses of a double chin. She gave off a powerful odor of perfume and whiskey.

"Brandy drinker, eh?" the woman said.

"That's right."

"Make mine another scotch and soda." As she watched the bartender moving away to fix the drinks, she said, "Here I am, old enough to be your mother. It's funny, isn't it? It's a funny world."

"Isn't it?"

"You don't live around here, do you?"

"No."

"I didn't think you did." She looked at him intently. "How old do you think I am?" she asked.

"Oh, I don't know."

"Make a guess."

"Thirty-eight or nine."

"You're all right!" she said, giving him a clap on the back that nearly sent him flying off the stool. "Thirty-eight or nine!" She laughed and nudged the man with the bow tie. "He thinks I'm thirty-eight!" she screamed into his ear.

"?"

"Thirty-nine!" she shouted. "He thinks I'm thirty-nine!"

"Can't hear you."

"Let it go," she said. She turned to William. "Deaf as a post," she informed him. "I'm forty-seven and I'll bet you I look it. I don't kid myself any. Not me." The bartender put the drinks down. Leaning over, the woman whispered, "I keep on the edge all the time. Just over the edge a little, maybe. Get what I mean? I'm that way now."

She stared at him so fixedly after this confession that William decided that some comment was necessary. "It's a good thing to do," he said guardedly, fingering his glass.

"Good thing!" the woman exclaimed. "I have to do it! I have to! I'd go crazy otherwise!" Her beads rattled against each other. "You don't know!"

she said. "Look at my hand." She held it out for him to examine. It trembled violently, a little too violently. "See?" she said. She gazed sadly for a moment at her reflection in the mirror and then dug around in her purse, producing a compact.

"Drink your brandy," she said, powdering her face. "I didn't mean to get started that way."

The pianist stood up and went out through the back door. The man who had been working the machine came over to the bar, a dollar bill in his hand.

"I'll take another dollar's worth of nickels, Dave," he said. "That thing can be beat." He went back to the machine, carrying a handful of coins. As he inserted one, he turned and said, "You know, I was in a place downtown the other night and the guy I was with cleaned out every damn thing out of one of these babies. Slickest thing you ever saw."

"What do you know?" the bartender said.

"Never saw anything like it."

The woman was frowning at William. "I don't see how you do it," she said.

"Do what?" He looked away from the crane, which was about to descend upon a kewpie doll in a crepe-paper dress. He wondered where Lund and the girl had gone.

"Drink brandy. Never could drink brandy. Guess a person has to have a taste for it. You go to the U?"

"Yes."

"I thought you did. Howard went there for a while.
What's your name?"

"Melvin Cathcart Lund."

"I used to know a man named Melvin," the woman
said dreamily. "He ran a grocery store in a little
town we used to live in in the western part of the
state. He used to give Howard fig newtons all the
time. My name's Mrs. Oatley."

"How do you do?"

"Have a brandy on me?"

"Not just now, thanks."

She smiled at him as the pianist returned. "How
about playing another piece for me, Eddie? Do you
know *The Kiss Waltz*? I love that."

"I just got through playing it a minute ago."

"Play it again, you bastard."

She descended from the stool and followed him
over to the piano, the merest suggestion of unsteadi-
ness in her walk. When he was seated, she leaned
against the piano, looking down at his hands. As
he played, tears came to her eyes, and she wiped
them away with a smooth white blue-veined hand.
She began to hum the tune in a soft voice, vaguely
flat, her body swaying. *"Telling us both what to do,"*
she sang. When he had finished, she looked at him
with gratitude and said, "That was grand. That was
simply grand. Give him a beer, Dave."

While they had been at the piano, a woman with

a baby had come in and seated herself at a table near the door. She bounced the baby up and down with one hand under it; with the other hand she patted it gently. "There, there," she said. The baby waved its white-mittened hands feebly towards its mother's face, clawing the air. Its knitted white cap, none too clean, had a bit of pink and blue ribbon drawn through it, which had come loose and now drooped over its forehead. Its mother removed the cap and blew on the top of its head, as though cooling soup.

"What a cute baby," Mrs. Oatley observed, after a brief glance at it. "Another scotch and soda, Dave."

William had another double brandy.

"I think *The Kiss Waltz* is lovely," she went on. "You know, though, it makes me so sad. Sometimes I think I shouldn't ever listen to it." She turned her head in the bartender's direction and said, "Fatten it up a little this time."

"Something I've been wanting to tell you," she said when her drink came. "I've been wanting to tell you ever since you first came in. It's the funniest thing."

"What is?"

"I can't get over it," she said. "But you look so much like my son Howard that it's kind of uncanny."

William lit a cigarette. "Really?"

"Even the way you do things!"

"Like what?"

"The way you light your cigarettes. It's just like Howard!" She reached for her purse. "Let me show you!"

William did not like the idea of looking like Howard Oatley. He rubbed his eyes. He should be back at the Esterlings, correcting papers. He looked across the room. The man operating the crane was still putting in nickels. William felt drowsy and incapable of moving. In the mirror his face seemed to belong to someone else.

Mrs. Oatley had taken something from her purse. "Just look at this!" she said, handing him a small snapshot, worn and smelling of face powder. It showed a young man in his early twenties, wearing a polo shirt and white trousers, posed before a truck marked: *Horowitz Fish Market.* "*If It Swims, We Have It.*" The camera had been pointed more towards the sun than away from it, and Howard's face was indistinct; but it wore the confident expression of one who is pleased with the knowledge that his picture is being taken.

No person, William thought, could look less like himself. He felt relieved; for a moment his own personality had been in jeopardy. He pretended to study the snapshot intently, marveling at the unusual resemblance. There was a dog in the picture. It was a white dog that had not been bathed in some time. "That's Buddy," Mrs. Oatley informed him, pointing out the dog. "He got run over."

"Too bad."

"He was such a nice, friendly dog, but he barked at cars all the time."

He handed the picture back to her. "Nice," he said.

"And don't you look like Howard, though?" She looked at the picture herself. There was writing on the back of it, dark blue ink in a female hand.

He tried to attract the bartender's attention to buy cigarettes, but Mrs. Oatley was talking to him about Howard. He had been such a cute little boy, she told him, and then after Mr. Oatley had died—a heart attack had taken him during a movie one night— Howard had become sullen, just sullen about things, she didn't know how to account for it, and he got to running around with girls, girls Mrs. Oatley didn't know the faintest thing about, staying out late nights and some nights not coming home at all. And then the first thing she knew Howard was married to some girl she didn't know a thing about. It had just about broken his mother's heart! If she could only have gotten her hands on that little tramp that had taken her Howard away from her! She'd give a lot to have done that. Oh, he didn't know what that girl was doing to her boy!

William suddenly realized that Mrs. Oatley was very drunk indeed.

"God," she was saying reverently. Her eyes were frighteningly large. "That's what we need, Melvin: God!"

"My name's William," said William.

She began to shout enthusiastically about God, about getting the spirit of Him into one's heart. The deaf man in the bow tie began to show signs of life at this point. "All right, Lillian," he said. "Come on now."

She was reluctant to go. She held on to William so tenaciously that the deaf man had a considerable struggle getting her out of the place and into a taxi. When he dragged her through the door, she was screaming about God and His love, about getting the spirit of love for Him into one's heart.

William had a small brandy and said goodnight to the bartender. He had lost his sense of direction and found difficulty in coordinating the movements of his legs. After he had walked several blocks, the feeling began to grow on him that he was being followed. He stopped and looked back. A street-lamp glowed at the end of the block. Otherwise it was very dark and alarmingly quiet. In the distance a clock was striking midnight.

He went on, quickening his steps. In the middle of the next block he turned and saw a man whom he thought he recognized as the pianist, dodging into the shadows.

William ran across the street, stumbling and bruising his knee. All the houses nearby were dark. As he stood up, he saw a figure rushing toward him, his arm upraised. William put up his arm to ward off the blow; then something that felt like a piece of lead pipe struck him on the top of his head.

When he awoke, the sun was shining. He was acutely conscious of a splitting headache and great thirst. His teeth felt gummy and around the rims of his eyeballs acid seemed to be eating. He felt gingerly of his head. There was a moderately large bump and some blood.

He was lying among some poisonous-looking weeds in a hollow of a vacant lot. Across the street was a warehouse where men in overalls were loading a truck. He discovered the top of a coffee can nearby and tried to examine his wound in it, but it was unsatisfactory as a mirror. His clothes were not bad, however. Feeling in his pockets as he stood up, he verified what he had suspected: all the money he had had with him, except for a quarter he found a few feet away, was gone.

He combed his hair and brushed off his clothes. In a restaurant a few blocks distant he washed and was relieved to see, in a wavy mirror, that the bump did not show. He drank a great deal of tomato juice for his breakfast.

It was nearly noon. He used the dime he had left over to take a streetcar back to the Esterlings. The sun hurt his eyes. Across the aisle from him two children were engaged in poking sticks at a canary they had in a cage.

He had to walk four blocks to get home. The town was crowded with persons coming into town for a football game that afternoon, and he barely escaped being run over by a man who wore a large yellow carnation and leaned out of the car to yell derisively at William after missing him by inches. A bloated-looking girl beside him availed herself of the opportunity to leer and wave a pennant at him.

In front of the house Mr. Esterling was shaking a can and applying a yellow powder to the Pekinese. The dog looked strangely haggard and worn, as though it had gone through some shattering experience.

Mr. Esterling looked up. "Didn't get in last night, eh?"

"No."

"There was a long distance call for you," Mr. Esterling went on, holding the dog firmly as it attempted to escape. "A Miss Frances Hyatt, I believe."

William felt suddenly as though someone had struck him in the pit of the stomach. He went in the house. Mrs. Esterling was just putting the telephone back on the stand.

"Oh, there you are!" she said. "I didn't know what to tell her. She just telephoned again. The fifth time since last night. You're to call Operator Five. A Miss Hyatt on long distance."

The odor of incense mingled with another unpleasant, but indefinable odor.

"Operator Five," William repeated mechanically; he picked up his mail and looked through it. A letter from his mother, a bill from a clothing store, a letter from Frances, a postcard inviting him to attend a meeting of a local poetry group—A Mrs. Henry Baechtold Wince was to discuss "Modern Poetry— What Is It?" on the following Wednesday.

Mrs. Esterling's expression was the feminine equivalent of the one worn by her husband when he had greeted William. No doubt they had been talking him over, he thought.

"I'll get in touch with her right away," he said. "I stayed with some friends last night. Should have called and told you where I was."

He felt her watching him as he climbed the stairs. He wondered if she could detect the bump on his head.

The air in his room was stale. He opened the windows. His cheeks felt red and puffy; rubbing his hand across his cheek, he realized he needed a shave in the worst way.

Scattered on his desk were some notes on an aspect of Crashaw he had scarcely touched upon in his thesis. He had put them there Thursday night, intending to spend the weekend working on an article to send to one of the scholarly journals. He gazed at them sadly.

He could not bring himself just then to open the letters. He walked down the hall to the bathroom

and rattled the knob. It sounded as though someone were playing Ping-pong in there. He stood for
a moment as though contemplating something. The
person within began to sing, in a loud and throaty
voice, a patriotic ballad. The Ping-pong noise ceased.

Returning to his room, he took off his shoes, listening to the happy baying noises created by a group
of college students on their way to the game. He
put on his slippers and went down to the telephone
and called the operator. While waiting for the call
to go through, he was assailed by nausea and felt
sweat crawling on the palms of his hands. His eyes
stung and the bump had begun to throb.

"Here's your party, Mr. Clay; go ahead, please,"
the operator said.

"Hello!" he said.   An empty buzzing sound came
from the receiver.

"Hello!" he said again. "Can you hear me?"

"Is that you, Bill? . . . Hello. Is Mr. Clay there?"

"This is Mr. Clay."

"Oh hello! I can hear you now. Bill, where *have*
you been?"

The Pekinese, now thoroughly powdered, entered
the hall and began to sniff intimately at William.
William gave it a slight kick. It cowered and then
left him for the living room, where it shook powder
all over the rug with much zest.

"You don't sound natural. Are you sick or something?"

"Oh, no. I'm fine, fine." He tried to get a genial quality into his voice. "I'm sorry you had such a lot of trouble getting me."

"Your voice sounds funny. Are you sure you're all right?"

"Oh, perfectly. I feel fine. I had to go out of town. A conference of teachers in the region." He felt sure, with mounting guilt, that the Esterlings were listening to him in the next room.

"Why didn't you write me about it? It must have come up awfully suddenly."

"Well, it did, rather, Frances. Oh, I'd known about it for a week or so. I just didn't think to write you about it. I just got back."

"It's funny you didn't write me about it."

"Well, I meant to, but I guess it slipped my mind." There was a pad by the telephone with some names and numbers written on it. Mrs. Parshall, William read in a blur, RE1375; Lena, PA0084; Mr. Munstenberg the horseradish man, WH7741.

"Did you go with that Devlin or whatever his name is?" Frances asked.

"He didn't go. He couldn't get away."

"What did you do?"

"Oh—just, you know, talked, discussed problems in the field."

There was a pause. He could hear the Esterlings moving closer to the door. Then she said, "Bill, do you miss me?"

My God, what have I been writing her all the time, he thought. He said, "You know I do. I'd give anything if I could see you."

"I get so lonesome here, I don't know what to do," she went on. "That Devlin doesn't sound like your type. I don't think I'd have much to do with him, Bill."

"Oh, he's all right," William said. "I'm so busy I don't see much of anyone."

"I suppose there are a lot of cute freshman girls that make eyes at you. I just know there are! Well, you just better not let me catch you looking at any of them, William Clay!"

William shuddered.

"Oh, Bill, I've been so lonesome and depressed. Mother went to the hospital yesterday. Her gall bladder again."

"That's a shame."

"And there doesn't seem to be anything much to do around here since you left. Are you sure you feel all right? Your voice sounds so funny."

"Three minutes," said the operator.

"Oh, Bill, darn it, I've got to stop now. Write me as often as you can. Your letters are so strange, sort of." Then she said, in an intense whisper, "You know I love you, Bill."

He started to reply in a similar vein, but the connection had been broken.

Who in the devil was Mr. Munstenberg, the horse-

radish man? He went up to the bathroom and was
violently ill.

EIGHT

Miss Bertha McVetchen had taught in the Department of English for fifteen years. Where she had
been and what she had done before coming to the
University were matters of curious speculation. She
had a series of degrees from a Canadian university,
now defunct, which where unquestionably documented
by diplomas on the wall of her office. Far more
interesting than these ugly engravings, however, was
the painting of her "old friend." It hung in her
apartment, near the screen which she hand covered
with cutouts from the dust jackets of books—an oil
painting of a handsome man in a black suit and
homburg hat. Whenever the eyes of one of Miss
McVetchen's guests fell upon it, and he inquired who
this gentleman was, she would merely smile nostal-
gically, looking away as though caught up by the
past in a not unpleasant rush of memory, and say,
"A friend only. An old, old friend." She displayed
a marked unwillingness to disclose anything more,
but it was a routine she undoubtedly relished. Some
persons had been so unkind as to suggest that Miss

McVetchen had purchased a portrait of a stranger so as to surround her life with mystery and an aura of lost but still cherished romance.

Miss McVetchen loved to give parties, and for years they were extremely popular. Her apartment became the meeting place for those who considered themselves the town's most advanced set, and, during a period in the 1920's when her popularity was at its height, evenings would find her rooms filled with people drinking her warm, impotent cocktails and discussing Elinor Wylie, Joseph Hergesheimer, Carl Van Vechten, Robert Frost, James Branch Cabell and other writers whose names it was important to repeat knowingly then. There would be heated arguments over Joyce, Gertrude Stein, Josephine Baker (whom one of her group had actually talked to for a few moments in Paris), Charlie Chaplin, Eliot, and the current issues of *Vanity Fair* and *The Ameican Mercury*. The problem of the artist in America was a favorite topic. One of Miss McVetchen's coterie, an instructor named Ralph Cumberland, had even gone so far as to publish something. It was a short story which had been given "two stars" by Mr. Edward J. O'Brien in his yearly anthology. The story, which concerned a woman on an Iowa farm who went insane, was rich in details relating to the prairie wind, oaths expressed by the crude hired hand, and featured intimate descriptions of wallowing hogs. Permeated as it was with the spirit of a stark regionalism, it was considered somewhat grim by a few members of the set, as most of whom, by 1936, became fellow travelers or members of the Communist Party. Mr. Cumberland later got his Ph. D. at Yale and committed suicide a few years afterwards in South Dakota. Speculations regarding his motives for suicide made conversation easy for weeks.

The popularity of Miss McVetchen's parties died slowly; then the arrival of Mrs. Diego Shanahan practically put an end to them. The very name of Mrs. Diego Shanahan, so outlandish and intriguing, alone might have attracted swarms of guests to her home. Such added interest was quite superfluous, however, for Mrs. Shanahan, who had moved from the East for her health, had a great deal of money, a huge home that eclipsed the appeal of Miss McVetchen's basement apartment, lavish generosity, and a vast supply of excellent scotch. It is not difficult to understand, bearing all this in mind, why few people went to Miss McVetchen's any more, and why they embraced the hospitality of Mrs. Diego Shanahan.

William sat on the edge of his bed reading the evening paper. A week had gone by since he had been slugged. The bump had disappeared. For William the past week had been filled with little of a pleasant nature: disruptions, eyestrain, fitful exasperation, and insufficient sleep. He was realizing, with growing dismay, that the time it took to prepare adequately the lecture for his first class left little time for the others. The task of disciplining the increasingly unruly and restive members of 101g was, in itself, an agonizing experience. He began to regard his older colleagues with envy. In going over the same ground for so many years, he reflected, most of them would have found it possible to repeat their lectures, complete with the well-known jokes with which they enlivened them, at any time and without the slightest thought.

He looked up from the paper, brooding on these matters and listening to the pianist next door as he or she started on a Czerny exercise. He was waiting for Devlin to pick him up. They were going to Mrs. Diego Shanahan's.

Devlin arrived promptly. He was wearing a new tweed suit and smoking a cigar.

"Sorry I had to kill your landlady's Pekinese," he said.

"My God, what happened?"

"You heard that yelping just before I came up, didn't you? The beast lunged at me and I let him have it. With this," he said, making his hand into a fist and displaying a large ring. "Poor little blighter. Better off dead, though." He grinned.

"There for a minute I thought you had."

"Merely jesting."

"Sure?"

"Absolutely." Devlin extracted a bottle from his pocket. "Better make use of this. The cocktails that Bertha McVetchen ladles out merely make one feel the need of the bathroom."

"Are we going there?"

"Oh, I forgot to tell you. I ran into her in the hall this afternoon and she insisted I bring you over. I said we could only come for a little while. We won't stay long. I told her you and I were collaborating on an article on Carlyle's loss of manhood."

"I've never been convinced that Carlyle *was* impotent."

"Well, I had to say something, and I think she was pleased." Devlin extended the bottle and shook it at William.

"Not me," said William.

"No?"

"No."

"Come, come. You'll thank me for it one day."

"Really, I don't want any. I was so damned sick last weekend I thought I was going to pass out."

"Just as you say," Devlin said, looking somewhat hurt. He began to put the bottle back in his pocket, thought better of it and had a rather stiff one. He stood looking at the bottle before replacing it. "And that reminds me. You haven't told me yet how you made out with Janet Eliot."

William did not reply. His look, meant for nothing in particular, was taken by Devlin as a slight leer.

Devlin drew down the corners of his lips, raised one eyebrow, and made a clucking noise with his tongue. "You don't say. Your silence moves me. But I see she has taken a powder on you, as I instruct my students to say on every occasion. You've seen the evening paper?"

"I was looking at it." William picked it up from the bed.

"Peruse this," said Devlin, opening it to an inside page on which a picture of Janet was displayed. She was wearing a very revealing bathing suit and was sitting on a sunny beach under a striped umbrella. She smiled tantalizingly, like a model in a toothpaste advertisement, at a young man beside her. The young man had a Coca-Cola bottle in his hand and was quite hairy. His name, according to the caption, was Roger Snyder III. The picture was taken at Palm Beach.

It depressed William. He folded the paper and put it on the bed. "She photographs well," he said.

"Very well indeed. Shall we go?"

William was moderately relieved to see that Ming, the Pekinese, was alive and standing at the bottom of the stairs, regarding them stupidly. Under ordinary circumstances, the dog merely annoyed him. Devlin stood in the doorway for a moment and gave the dog a menacing look before going out. They walked down the sidewalk, kicking through the dry leaves that had fallen, and got in Devlin's car. Next door, the pianist played Czerny with heavy irritability.

"Ah, crisp October nights!" Devlin exclaimed, pulling on the old gloves he wore when driving. "It brings back my youth, my fine lost youth: the frost on the pumpkin, the fodder in the shock, lovely young girls offering me their slim white bodies as we roasted chestnuts around a roaring fire. How this brings it back! Autumn! I can taste those chestnuts yet! Wormy, and very unpleasant. It all brings it back, let me tell you, William!" Devlin shifted the gears. "Yes, indeed," he said, belching slightly.

The steps leading down to Miss McVetchen's apartment were very steep. Frequently they were covered with potted plants, kitchen utensils and cleaning equipment, and it required definite skill to get to the bottom without mishap. Several of Miss McVetchen's acquaintances had injured themselves badly when, inadvertently losing control of themselves near the top, they hand plunged down the flight, knocking against trowels, rakes and ice-cream freezers in their descent.

Devlin cautioned William about these perils. "You don't mind taking your life in your hands, I hope," he said at the top. "Now, if you'll just step where I do, I'll lead the way. If you see me going, just

stand frozen in your tracks, and we'll send someone to get you."

In the darkness they cautiously felt their way.

"I just passed a pair of roller skates," Devlin called
back. "Careful they don't throw you."

Finally arriving at the bottom, they went on, past
the furnace and the coal bin and an immense collection of meters on the wall, to a door painted robin's
egg blue. Miss McVetchen's card was tacked on it.
Devlin knocked.

"Hello, Bertha," he said when she opened the door
and let them in. "You ought to have medals to award
people who finally get down here. Why don't you
get the landlord to take out those stairs and install
a rope?"

"Mr. Devlin, you're irrepressible!" Miss McVetchen
exclaimed, turning her eyes, with the wrinkles around
them decorated with greasepaint as always, first upon
him and then William. "I'm so glad you could come!"
she said to him, shaking his hand. "I haven't had a
chance to have a good talk with you since you came,
not since that first day, at the meeting! You just
put your things here in the closet and come in!"

She ushered them into the room that contained
the picture of her elderly friend.

"Here's Nelson Castleman!" said Miss McVetchen.

She was referring to a man who was sitting in a
rocking chair by the window. He wore a shirt the
color of lemons and appeared lost in thought. He

was about thirty-eight and looked like the sort of person who always orders the fruit cup on the sixty-five cent dinner.

"Nelson and I were just trying to remember how the *Anvil Chorus* goes," Miss McVetchen explained, for the man had begun to hum tensely, frowning to himself.

"Why?" said Devlin in a low voice. He greeted Castleman and introduced him to William.

Nelson Castleman nodded in a preoccupied way. "The whole chorus sings and then a man comes in," he said, looking up at their hostess.

"What man is that, Nelson?" Miss McVetchen said.

"George," Devlin said, sitting down. "A man named George."

Nelson Castleman was not amused. He frowned at Devlin and then, seized with a sudden fervor, began to beat on the arm of his chair and sing, employing the monosyllables of baby talk, what might have passed as the *Anvil Chorus. "Da! Da!* Da *da* da *da!"* he sang.

"Oh, fine," said Devlin to William, who had unknowingly seated himself in the most uncomfortable chair in the room.

"That's it!" said Miss McVetchen.

Nelson Castleman was now smiling happily. "Funny how things come to you," he said. "You know, I'll tell you something. I really have a very bad memory. Can't remember telephone numbers or addresses or things like that for the life of me. I took one of those courses in improving your memory once, but it didn't do the slightest bit of good. A lot of my friends got a lot of help from it, but it didn't seem to work for me." Again he hummed the opening bars of the *Anvil Chorus*. "My mind's essentially creative, I suppose that's the reason."

Miss McVetchen, attempting to appear fascinated with Nelson Castleman's revelations and at the same time solicitous of her other guests, turned to Devlin and William. "May I get you a drink."

While she was in the kitchen, Nelson Castleman told them more about his memory. They had to listen rather a long time. "It's the essentials that count," he informed them. "I never let the essentials escape me."

"A good rule," said Devlin, picking up a book and reading the title as though enthralled.

"You in the English Department at the U?" Castleman asked William.

"Yes."

"Where'd you go to school?"

William told him.

Castleman nodded as though he was well acquainted with it and gave it his approval. "Friend of mine used to teach there," he said as Miss McVetchen returned with four glasses on a tray.

"What have you there?" said Devlin. "A tasty fruit punch?"

Miss McVetchen giggled. "Oh, Mr. Devlin, you always make fun of my drinks. I know you think I make them awfully weak, but it's just not good for you to drink it straight the way you do."

"Drink it *straight*?" said Devlin in a horrified voice. "I have no idea what you're talking about, Bertha."

"I can't take much," Castleman said to William. "Bad for my heart." He put his hand over this organ in a thoughtful way.

"Don't you think Mr. Devlin is simply terrible, the way he goes on?" Miss McVetchen said to William, offering him a glass.

"Yes, I had this friend who used to teach there," Castleman said. "Winston Gunzell. He was probably before your time. Taught biology."

Above them, someone began to jump about in a frenzy, shaking the ceiling considerably.

"The new people up there have a nephew who has fits," Miss McVetchen explained.

"A large person, evidently," Devlin said.

"Yes, quite large."

"One of my students had a fit in the classroom the other day," said Devlin. "It worked in very nicely, as I happened to be discussing the Russian novelists at the time."

"Listen!" said Miss McVetchen as the noise ceased. "Do you hear someone on the stairs?"

They listened. The whole building was suddenly quiet.

"I don't hear anything," Nelson Castleman said.

"I guess it mustn't be anything. I thought maybe it might be Mordecai Boepple. He said he'd probably be here tonight."

"Oh?" William said.

"You'll like Mordecai Boepple, I feel sure."

"You didn't know Winston, did you?" Castleman said to William.

"No."

"Did some very interesting work on the digestive system of the codling moth."

Devlin had managed, after putting his glass on the floor by his chair, to remove the bottle from his pocket and unscrew the cap. Watching Bertha McVetchen with a cautious eye to make sure she was not watching him, he poured several ounces of whiskey into the glass. After completing this act and returning the bottle to his pocket, he smiled brightly at her. "Lovely weather we're having, isn't it?"

"Oh, lovely!"

"I think it's lovely."

"How are you enjoying your work by this time, Mr. Clay?" she asked.

"Very much."

"Poor boy, you have 101g though, don't you?"

"They make it rather difficult."

"Don't I know!" she said. "Poor, poor things! They should never be admitted to the University in the first place. Their poor minds are simply not capable."

"Trying to keep them quiet is about all I can handle," William said, pleased to have an opportunity to speak of his difficulties. "What they need is a football coach, not an English instructor."

"I know," said Miss McVetchen, nodding. "I know."

"Haven't seen Winston Gunzell in years," Castleman said. "Think he's working for the government now. You didn't know anyone there in the biology department at all?"

"No one," William said.

"Everyone there was very much interested in the codling moth at the time."

"Understand you have a new book coming out," Devlin said to Castleman. "What's this one about?"

"It's called *The Boy's Book of Camera Craft*," said Castleman.

"A fine title."

"Do you think so?"

"Absolutely."

"I couldn't decide between it and *The Boy's Book of Photography*."

"I don't think there's any doubt but that you picked the right one."

"I'm working on the next one now," Castleman said with a smile. "*The Boy's Book of Carpentry*."

"That should fill a need," said Devlin, lighting a cigar. "It really astounds me the way you turn them out, Nelson. How many have there been? Twelve?"

"Fourteen! I try to do three a year. With what I write for the magazines, it brings in a good income. Get up every morning at seven, start writing at eight and keep at it until five-thirty. Regular hours. That's what you've got to do. Of course I know you fellows, with all your literary notions, look down on the kind of work I do—"

"Why, not at all!" Devlin said.

"Oh yes you do! I know the way you feel! I've heard you talk!"

"Don't be ridiculous," said Devlin.

There was a noise from the bathroom, and a gnarled little woman, carrying a black oilcloth bag, emerged and walked through the room.

"Goodnight, Miss McVetchen," she said.

"Goodnight, Mrs. Waterbury. Did you get the bones for your dog?"

"Yes, thank you. Goodnight." She went out and closed the door and they listened to her feeling her way up the treacherous stairs.

"My little cleaning woman," Miss McVetchen explained.

William nodded understandingly.

"I do wish Mordecai Boepple would come. I'd like to have you meet him. A couple of others were coming, but at the last minute they called and said they couldn't."

"*Who* is Mordecai Boepple?" William asked.

Devlin said, "I'll tell you someone you ought to

write about, Nelson."

"Who?" Nelson Castleman said. He was still ruffled, for he had been brooding about the lack of respect shown for his work by such persons as Devlin.

"Athanasius Kircher."

"Never heard of him."

"What!" Devlin exclaimed. "Never heard of Athanasius Kircher?"

"No."

"I'm surprised to hear that, Nelson. For it should be through you that the youth of America should learn of him. Go up to the average American boy and say, 'What do you know about Athanasius Kircher?' and what do you get? I'll tell you what you get. Nothing. A dull, glazed look, if you're lucky."

"Who was this guy?" Castleman asked.

"I can see the book already. *The Boy's Book of Athanasius Kircher.*"

"Would you mind telling me just who he was?" Castleman said, somewhat testily.

"Not in the least. Athanasius Kircher was a physicist, optician, Orientalist, musician, mathematician virtuoso, physician—probably the first man to employ the microscope in investigating the causes of diseases. He is the author of a work on curing the bite of the Tarantula spider by music. He was a Jesuit priest and one of the most versatile geniuses and active spirits of his time."

"Never heard of him," said Castleman.

"He is known as the inventor of the magic lantern. He was the first man to mention physiological colors, and issue charts of the oceanic currents." Devlin looked at Castleman for a moment. "You keep Athanasius Kircher in mind, Nelson. He might be the very thing to fall back on during some sterile period."

"I don't know, Devlin. Doesn't sound like quite the thing for my readers."

"I *do* wish Mordecai Boepple would come," said Miss McVetchen.

Devlin looked at his watch. "Is it that late? I had no idea. I'm afraid, Bertha, that we must run along."

"Oh, do you have to?" Miss McVetchen said. "Why, it isn't late at all! I do wish you'd stay."

"We have this work we must get at," said Devlin.

"You haven't stayed a minute! . . . Mr. Clay, I want you to feel free to drop in any time. I like to get to know the younger members of the department better. And I'm *very* interested in what Mr. Devlin tells me about this work you and he are doing on Mr. Carlyle."

William thanked her for the drink. He and Devlin had to stand outside the door for some time while she completed a lengthy farewell.

Going up the stairs, William stumbled on some blunt object and sprained his leg slightly. He limped out to the car.

"That place gives me the creeps," Devlin said. "Hurt yourself much?"

"Hardly at all."

"Good. Only rarely does one leave without some sort of injury." Devlin drew on his gloves and peered at the dash to insert the key. "And now—Mrs. Diego Shanahan's."

NINE

It was a large red house of dubious architectural interest. Stone lions, somewhat the worse for wear, guarded each side of the walk, and statuary was strewn about the grounds. The house had stood empty for several years following the death of its builder, a Mr. Wilson; and had been known, during the period of its vacancy, as "Wilson's Folly." Now it was referred to, by disapproving townspeople and tight-lipped faculty wives who drove past, as "the place where that Mrs. Shanahan lives."

That evening, all the lights in the house were on except those in one bedroom on the fourth floor, where a Mr. Hunter, one of the guests, had been carried to sleep it off. Following his usual practice, Mr. Hunter had passed out a scant ten minutes after his arrival. His sense of timing was admittedly unbeatable. Yellow light from the windows flooded the lawn as William and Devlin got out of the car and went up the walk to ring the bell.

They were admitted by Mrs. Shanahan herself. Encased in a wine-colored evening gown and wearing pearl earrings the size of cough drops, her straight hair done up in a bun at the back of her neck, she had the look of a person who has just finished a heavy meal and finds difficulty in moving about, yet manages somehow to preserve and exude a native heartiness.

"So you're William Clay," she said, extending a bulky and naked arm on which the Shanahan collection of bracelets fell jangling. She had a powerful handshake which caused William to cringe. "Somebody or other was telling me you were playing around with one of the Eliot girls. Which one was it?"

"Janet," Devlin said.

"Oh, yes, yes, Janet," she said vaguely. "That's right. The other girl is married, isn't she? Darling girls. But then you never know, do you? What I mean to say is, they're a very nice family, of course; trace their ancestry back to Richard the Lion-Hearted, but my personal feeling is that none of them have any essential character. I hope you don't mind my speaking frankly. No *essential* character. Do you know what I mean, Christopher?"

Devlin had been staring at a small brown protuberance on Mrs. Shanahan's neck. He nodded his head. "I think I do. Yes."

"But do you?"

"I think I do."

"I wonder." Mrs. Shanahan leaned forward and felt of the lapel of William's suit. "That's nice material," she said. "Very nice. My husband, my second husband, that is, Mr. Jamison, had a suit very much like that. He was a construction engineer, you know. Of course, I've never felt that I fully understood men. I've been married three times and you'd think that by this time I'd have a *little* understanding. But, you know, understanding doesn't come from mere *quantity* of experience. Oh, not at all! Not at all! Understanding, at the last, I'm afraid, eludes us all. At least, it eludes *me*. I have often thought—Oh, hello, Marvin. Come and meet these friends of mine. I guess you know Christopher Devlin."

She had spoken to a tall, redheaded man with a large Adam's apple and slender hands named Marvin Herendeen. He was smoking a cigarette in a holder, and acknowledged the introduction to William by waving it slightly and bowing.

"Show them where to put their things, Marvin," Mrs. Shanahan said, poking at several loosened strands of hair in an attempt to imbed them in the bun. "I've got to see about something." She seemed to contract slightly as she moved away.

They deposited their wraps on a four-poster bed

in a room on the second floor. There was a Matisse
on the wall. William did not have time to inspect it
carefully. Coming down red-carpeted stairs, Marvin
Herendeen complained of Mr. Hunter, the man who
had passed out. "He's getting to be a dreadful bother,"
Herendeen said. "Every party the same thing. I
don't know why Annabelle keeps asking him."

There were ten or eleven people in the high-ceil-
inged, paneled room at the end of the hall. One of
them, a blond youth in a dinner jacket, was playing
The Man I Love on a grand piano with much lowering and flinching of his shoulders, while a slight,
dark girl who sat beside him on the bench, smiled
toothily up at him. Everyone was drinking and talking.
Someone pressed a very large glass into William's
hand as he was led around the room by Herendeen
to be introduced. A few moments later, deposited
in a chair, he found himself between a man and a
woman whose names he had not caught. He tasted
the drink, which seemed to have been concocted with
a half pint of rum as its base, and was attended
with the sort of dread he experienced in the classroom when a student whose name he could not recall
raised his hand. As he looked around the handsome room with a mixture of attraction and repul-
sion at these strangers, who had been presented to
him in such hurried succession, they all seemed as
anonymous and alien as the people one observes on
trains or streetcars. He had another drink.

"All I said was," the man in the chair next to him said, leaning over toward the woman and scowling, "was that she had very beautiful breasts."

He had intruded into a quarrel. The man, whom he was startled to recognize as the surly and disheveled blond companion of the girl at the Bryant Hotel, looked at William and said by way of explanation, "The little woman and I were just having a slight disagreement."

His wife smiled wanly at William. She was a very plain and rather poorly dressed girl, with pale skin and what William thought was an expression marked by patience and suffering. Her hands, he noticed, were rough, and she wore a plain gold-band wedding ring.

"You act as though it was something that isn't to be discussed in mixed company," her husband said to her. "If women don't want them seen and talked about, why don't they cover them up or something? Why don't they put shoe boxes over them?" He borrowed a cigarette from William. "I didn't catch your name."

"Clay."

"My name's Thompson. Couldn't understand a word that mush-mouthed Herendeen said." Thompson's glass was empty and he held it out and agitated it for his wife to see. "How about getting me another one?" he said.

She acquiesced to this demand with very good grace.

William observed, as she left them, that she walked as though her feet were tired.

"Female jealousy can be a maddening thing," Thompson said, going through his pockets for matches and finally accepting William's. "That is, if it wasn't so amusing, so silly. I suppose you've read *Madame Bovary*, by Gustave Flaubert."

"Yes," said William.

"Then you know what I mean. Gustave Flaubert was a very great writer."

"I quite agree with you."

"And *Madame Bovary* was indubitably his masterpiece."

"I think there is no argument."

"He knows women."

"Yes."

"Forward and backward."

William nodded.

"Annabelle Shanahan's a remarkable person, don't you think?"

"I've only just met her."

"She's a remarkable person," Thompson said, dropping cigarette ashes on his vest as his wife returned with a drink for him. "A remarkable person." He took the glass, tilted his head, and actively expressed his approval of the beverage by drinking half of it. Lowering the glass reluctantly, he expelled his breath and wiped his mouth with the back of his hand. "Yes, damned good drinks." He stood up. "Pardon me; there's a tune I want to ask Norwin to play." He left them and went over to the piano.

There was a silence, during which William studied a man across the room who was drawing a diagram on the back of an envelope and apparently illustrating some tactical manoeuvre to a stout woman.

"You've moved here recently?" Mrs. Thompson inquired.

"Yes, just this Fall."

"I saw you with Christopher Devlin. I suppose you teach at the University?"

"Yes."

"I teach, too."

"Really?"

"Junior high school."

"That must be wearing," he said. "Does your husband teach?"

"Oh, no! He's a painter."

William had a vision of the man on a ladder, wearing white coveralls and a cap with a bill.

"He does oils and watercolors. That is, he used to; he hasn't painted a picture for a long, long time. He isn't well, you know. Chester doesn't look it, but he's really very delicate. He's had several nervous breakdowns. Annabelle Shanahan's bought one of his pictures."

"How interesting."

"Would you like to see it?"

"Very much."

She took him through a corridor and into another room, a sort of den or study. Bookcases covered two of the walls; the others were hung with paintings. There was a thick rug on the floor. A prematurely bald young man was sitting before a fireplace with an empty glass in his hand. There was a St. Bernard asleep on the hearth.

"Hello," the young man said, looking up at them glassily. "I'm just sitting here watching the flames flicker. You see that St. Bernard dog?"

They looked at it.

"I kidnapped him. Belongs to the Alpha Phis. Jeez, I bet they're worrying themselves sick wondering what's become of their dog." He stared at William. His eyes were blue and watery. "What's your name?" he asked.

"William Clay."

The young man sucked in his cheeks. "You want me to tell you something?"

"Of course."

"The Alpha Phis are a bunch of cunts." He looked at the animal wistfully and leaned over to pat it. He had difficulty in keeping his balance and nearly fell from the chair. The dog did not awaken. "This dog's my pal," he told them. Suddenly he went limp and closed his eyes.

"I think I've seen him around on the campus," William said.

"The St. Bernard?"

"No, the man."

"He was at one of Annabelle's parties last winter. He was trying to sell people subscriptions to *The American Boy* or something. Chester almost got in a fight with him." Mrs. Thompson sighed. "But I wanted to show you the painting. It's really the best thing Chester's ever done."

It was a large portrait of a girl sitting on a blue chair against a yellow wall. William stared at it for a long time without saying anything.

"Don't you think it's good?" Mrs. Thompson asked.

"Yes, wonderful."

"I think it's good. The one Chester tried to paint of me he couldn't even finish. It's stored away in a closet at home. He said he couldn't paint me."

"It's a wonderful likeness," William said.

"Oh, do you know Dorothy?"

"No. I've just seen her a couple of times."

"Well, she'll probably be here tonight."

"Here?"

"Oh yes, she's sure to come."

"It's strange. It's quite amazing," he said. "The first night I was in town I saw her."

Mrs. Thompson sat down and looked at the fire, which had begun to burn low. "Chester worked very hard on it."

"He's caught her eyes exactly. She has wonderful eyes, don't you think?"

"They're very nice."

"Dorothy, did you say? What's her last name?"

"Bruce."

William was having trouble with his hands, and his heart was beating violently. He found an ashtray for Mrs. Thompson and sat beside her on the couch, restraining a compulsion to turn and feast his eyes once more on the painting. A log on the fire cracked and sparks fell on the hearth. The St. Bernard breathed with heavy asthmatic effort, his legs jerking. The dog's abductor had begun to snore. A wind had come up while they had been talking and the windows were streaked with rain.

"We're going to have a storm, I guess," said Mrs. Thompson. "I certainly hope there's someone here who can take us home. We don't have a car now, since Chester had the accident."

William noticed the wrinkles around her eyes and a mark across the bridge of her nose. She must wear glasses, he thought, and pictured her seated at a desk in the junior high school building. At this point, he was on the verge of suggesting that they join the others when, glancing up, he saw Chester Thompson standing in the doorway. He remained there for a moment, wagging his head back and forth as though his collar gave him discomfort. He did not say anything but came into the room and inspected the man in front of the fireplace. He lifted one of his arms and let it drop. "That's the same guy I tangled with here before, isn't it, Doris?"

"Yes."

"Unpleasant bastard. Whose dog?"

"He said it belonged to the Alpha Phis," said William.

Thompson gave William a long look that seemed to imply that this could not possibly be so. He sat on the arm of the couch and ran his fingers through his hair. "I knew an Alpha Phi once. Helen Babcock. Took her out a couple of times, but I couldn't get her to come across. I gave her the old gather-the-rosebuds stuff but it was strictly from Alaska. You know me. Then I got tough with her. I didn't get to first base either way, and everybody'd told me she was a pushover, too. I wonder what ever happened to that gal. I'd like to have painted her. She had an interesting behind, I must say."

William glanced at Mrs. Thompson. Her expression was that of a veteran poker player. He was filled with distaste by this revelation of the painter's, which he could not reconcile with his artistic bent; for William had fancied that most painters were not like this at all—they were something like neo-Humanists, the Iowa neo-Humanists perhaps. William's acquaintance with painters was limited to a long- deceased aunt, who, in her youth, had painted grapes and apples on china.

"You come in here to see that canvas of Dorothy?" Thompson asked.

"Yes."

"How do you like it?"

"I like it."

"Well I don't," Thompson said bluntly. "Sometimes I don't think it's worth a goddamn. One of these days, though, I'm going to paint something that'll really knock their ears down."

"Chester, you know it's a fine painting," his wife said.

"I don't know anything of the sort. Don't be butting in. And don't tell me I'm wrought up, for Christ's sake."

"I didn't."

"You looked like you were going to." To William he said, "If there's one thing I'm sure of, it's that I'm the best judge of my own stuff. I suppose you're one of these boys who think the only good painters left are the ones that live in Europe."

William was not permitted to reply to this accusation, for Thompson continued, "Cézanne is the only one of the whole bunch that had much on the ball. Picasso's nothing but a fake, and he's the best of the lot." He looked up at his own canvas and gazed at it for a time. "I don't know," he said. "Maybe it's not so bad, after all. I'm damned if I can make up my mind."

"You know it's good, Chester," his wife said.

He looked at her as though she were not there and said to William, "How about a cigarette professor?"

William gave him one and excused himself, mumbling that he had to get in touch with Devlin. He walked through the corridor, stopping for a moment at a mirror to adjust his tie and smooth his hair. In the large room several couples were dancing to the radio. Someone had spilled a drink on one of the rugs and a servant was attempting to repair the damage. In one corner, a group was playing a game with dice. The man who had drawn the diagram was showing it to Marvin Herendeen, who looked bored. Devlin was talking to Mrs. Shanahan.

Devlin said, "I was just telling Annabelle that someone ought to make a movie with Walter Abel, Clark Gable, and Betty Grable. There's money in it, I feel sure. Some producer ought to grab at it."

William looked around, hoping that Dorothy Bruce had arrived. He couldn't see her. "Mrs. Thompson has been showing me her husband's painting," he said.

"I *do* like that suit you're wearing," Mrs. Shanahan said. "Why didn't you bring Janet Eliot along with you? It's been ages since she's been to my house. She was here once with the most delightful man from Florida who did coin tricks." A servant carrying a tray full of drinks went by. Mrs. Shanahan stopped him and gave William and Devlin glasses. She said to the servant, "Go up and see if Mr. Hunter is getting along all right. He may need something."

"Yes, Mrs. Shanahan."

She turned to William. "Poor Mr. Hunter. What was it you were saying about a painting?"

"Chester Thompson's. The one you have."

"Yes, oh yes. It's quite good, isn't it? Quite good, I've always felt. Chester has lots of talent, but one can't depend on him at all. I thought once I might support him, but after that night when he tried to stab my butler, I've never felt quite the same about Chester. I didn't even invite him tonight, but of course I don't care particularly just as long as he doesn't try to knife anybody."

Devlin took a drink. "Abel, Gable, and Grable," he said. "The names have a strange and haunting appeal to me."

"Why did he want to stab your butler?" William asked.

"I haven't the faintest idea. I didn't mind so awfully because it turned out the butler was a kleptomaniac and I had to get rid of him anyway. You still haven't told me why you didn't bring Janet."

"She's in Florida, I understand."

"With that nice coin-trick man, I suppose."

"I don't think so."

Mrs. Shanahan wore a thoughtful look. "Clark Gable and Betty Grable," she said. "Who was the other one?"

William, with a premonition of excitement, turned slightly. Approaching them were Melvin Cathcart Lund and the girl named Dorothy Bruce. She was wearing a green evening gown that was cut very low. Her hair was faintly damp from the rain. William had never been so close to her and the universe seemed suddenly larger. She was even more beautiful, he felt, than the other times he had seen her. As they came near, Lund whispered something to her and she laughed softly in a way that agitated William. When they were introduced and he took her hand, she gave him a look from her gray-green eyes that was curious and alert and interested.

"I'd about given you two up," Mrs. Shanahan said, motioning wildly to a servant so that her bracelets raced up and down her arm.

"Dorothy had a rehearsal and I got tied up myself at the last minute," Lund said. He sounded very Harvard this evening. He nodded to William and Devlin with a marked lack of enthusiasm. "Then, of course, this storm came up."

"The strangest thing happened at the studio!" Dorothy Bruce said. "One of the announcers lost his voice just before we were going on the air. He just opened his mouth and nothing came out! Gee, it was the strangest thing! Well, we all just stood there for a couple of seconds, and then one of the musicians had enough presence of mind to take the script and read the announcement. It was just a few seconds, but it seemed like hours!"

"A state referred to in the medical profession as aphonia, I believe," said Devlin, helping himself from a new tray of drinks that had been brought and offering one of them to Dorothy Bruce.

"Is that what they call it?" she said. "No, thank you; I don't drink. I would like a Coke, though, if you have one, Annabelle."

"Have we any Cokes, Iams?" Mrs. Shanahan asked the servant.

"I beg your pardon, ma'am?"

"Coca-Colas. Have we any?"

"I think not, ma'am."

"Why don't you go out and get me a Coke, Melvin?" said Dorothy, taking him by the arm.

"That rain's coming down pretty hard. Wait until it lets up a bit."

William said, "Why don't you let me go? I'll be glad to."

"You're not afraid of the rain?"

"Not in the least."

"It seems like an awful imposition."

"It isn't at all."

"Take my car," said Devlin, giving William the keys.

Melvin Cathcart Lund was frowning. "Now, look here, Clay, you don't need to do that." He gave William the caricature of a smile. "I don't mind going at all. That rain *was* coming down rather hard, though, and we came in a taxi. Let me borrow your car, Devlin."

"Where's yours?"

"At the garage."

"Have you your driver's license?"

"I haven't it with me."

"One should always carry one's driver's license," said Devlin. "Sign of definite laxity on your part, Melvin. I think Clay had better go. He loves the rain. You *do* have your license, haven't you?"

"Yes."

"May I see it?" said Lund.

"Gee, I wish you wouldn't bother," Dorothy Bruce said. "I can get along perfectly well without a Coke."

"I would very much like to see it."

"I don't think that will be necessary," said Devlin.

Mrs. Shanahan, seizing upon a remark to break the tension, placed her hand on Devlin's arm and said, "Walter Abel! Now I remember! Does he have a mustache?"

"Yes."

"Plays district attorneys?"

"Now that you mention it, I believe that he does."

Mrs. Shanahan turned radiantly upon them. "Christopher has the most remarkable idea!" she announced. "He thinks someone ought to do a movie with Walter Abel and Clark Gable."

"*And* Betty Grable," said Devlin. "I should not like *her* to be omitted."

The man with the diagram came up and said, "Hello there, Lund. What do you know? Little thing I'd like to show you if you have a minute."

As Lund was led away, William said to Dorothy Bruce, "I'll get the Coke for you. It'll only take a minute."

He still had a vision of her smile as he went outside. It was a pouring rain. Running out to the car, he slipped and nearly lost his balance. The starter was not functioning and he spent some time looking under the front seat for the crank. He eventually located it under some empty beer bottles and a burlap sack. He stood in the downpour and attempted to insert the crank, but it soon dawned on him that it did not fit. He found another crank, one that fitted, in the storage compartment in the back. By the time he had the engine running, his clothes were soaked and he had begun to sneeze violently.

The car did not behave in a normal manner. It moved in spasmodic, irritable jerks and then, with a sudden unaccountable burst of speed, plunged madly ahead for several hundred feet before giving a warning cough that heralded the resumption of the jerking movement. This continued, to William's disturbance, all the way downtown, which was some distance from Mrs. Shanahan's neighborhood.

It was late, and the first drugstore he came to was closed. A dim light burned in the back of the place. He drove on down the street and parked in front of another drugstore. There was a cardboard cutout of a nurse in the window who held out a hot-water bottle invitingly. William went inside. The soda jerk, maneuvering a toothpick in his mouth, informed him that they did not carry Coca-Cola in bottles.

"I can mix one and put it in a carton," he offered.

"No, thank you," William said, looking down at his feet. A small pool of rainwater was forming there. He returned to the car. He had turned off the motor and was obliged to use the crank again.

He was shivering and his nose was beginning to run. He visited three places before he located a filling station on the outskirts of town that had Coca-Cola in bottles. Coming out, he found the engine was dead. He cranked for a long time without results, aided by the filling station attendant, who stood out of the rain and offered remarks of an encouraging nature.

Half an hour later, a car that stopped for gas towed him to a garage in town. It was another hour before Devlin's car was pronounced to be in running order by the garagemen. William was soaked to the skin. While the men worked, he sat on a box by a stove with a dirty blanket wrapped around him. He paid the bill and drove back to Mrs. Shanahan's.

No one answered when he rang the doorbell. His teeth chattered and he felt feverish. Opening the door, he went inside, carrying the bottles of Coca-Cola.

The large room was empty. There was a broken phonograph record on the floor and remnants of a cocktail sausage under a chair.

He went in the den, stepping on an olive pit in the hall. Devlin was sitting before the fire, feeding sandwiches to the St. Bernard.

"What did you do—fall in a lake?" he asked, looking up at William.

"Here are the Cokes," William said, putting them down. He was very pale.

"You'd better take those wet clothes off. God, how did you ever get so wet?" Devlin broke off a piece of sandwich and offered it to the dog.

"Where's Dorothy?"

Devlin frowned, as though trying to recollect something that had happened years before. "Oh, the whole bunch of them left. There was a report on the radio that an airplane crashed a few miles west of town and they all drove out to see the damage." He took another from a large pile near his arm. "Here, Edgar," he said.

"You think they'll be back?"

"It's most unlikely."

"I don't suppose she'll want these Cokes, then."

"No."

"I had to take your car to the garage."

"Which one?"

"It says 'We Never Sleep' on the front."

"What was the matter with it?"

"It wouldn't run."

This answer seemed to satisfy Devlin. "You pay them?" he asked.

"Yes."

"How much was it?"

"Five dollars."

"The complete car isn't worth that amount."

William stood looking at the Coca-Colas with a queer expression.

"Chester Thompson tried to pick a fight with Lund while you were gone," Devlin said.

William sat down.

"Nothing much came of it." Devlin wiped his hands on a napkin and poured some rum into a glass. "Did I ever tell you that Annabelle Shanahan has a sound-proof room on the third floor where she goes to play the kettledrums? It's kept very quiet; no one speaks of it. Seems to be sort of an orgy with her. She started all this about the time she began to have hot and cold flashes."

"Was she angry when I didn't come back with the Cokes?"

"Who? Annabelle?"

"Dorothy."

"For God's sake, Bill, take off those wet clothes. You look like you'd just been picked up by a life-boat. How long have you been that wet?

"I don't know, a couple of hours," William said in a weak voice.

"I think I'd better get you home."

"Would you mind?" William said, closing his eyes. His head rolled over to one side and, as he breathed, a remote rattling noise came from somewhere in the region of his chest.

Devlin sat looking at him for a moment. Then he drank the rum and called, "Iams!" Standing over William, he lifted the lid of his right eye, into which he peered with a faint shudder.

When the servant appeared, Devlin said, "Well, you see what we have to deal with."

"Yes, sir."

"You take his feet and I'll take his head."

"Yes, sir."

"If you don't mind."

They carried him to one of the upstairs bedrooms and began to undress him. William appeared to be unconscious. The St. Bernard followed them and sat watching them curiously.

"Complete the disrobing, Iams," Devlin directed, going down to the bathroom and turning on the hot water in the tub. When he came back, William had been undressed and wrapped in a woolen blanket. Iams was gathering the wet clothing together.

"I think I can manage from here on," Devlin said. He lifted William and carried him to the bathroom. William was mumbling to himself.

"Iams!" Devlin called over his shoulder.

"Yes, sir."

"Call Mrs. Shanahan's physician and tell him to come over at once."

"Very good, sir."

"Suggest that it's a matter of life and death."

He felt of the water several times before he was satisfied with its temperature. Then he lifted William and let him down in the tub. William opened his eyes and stared blankly at his friend. "Dorothy," he said.

"Take it easy," Devlin said. "You're going to be okay."

William closed his eyes again and slid down in the water. Devlin pulled him up and hung one of his arms over the side of the tub. He could hear Iams telephoning the doctor; he seemed to be experiencing some difficulty with the operator. Going to the head of the stairs after making sure that William was unlikely to immerse himself entirely, Devlin lighted the stub of a cigar and waited. The dog approached him from behind and put his nose in the palm of Devlin's hand. "What a fine dog you are, old chap," Devlin said. "I feel like reciting Senator Vest's oration."

"He's coming?" Devlin called over the bannister when he heard Iams hanging up.

"At once, sir."

"Good. I'm staying up here. Will you bring me the bottle of rum I left in the den? If it's nearly gone, you'd better get me a fresh one. Oh yes, and something to read, if you don't mind. See if you can locate the plays of John Webster for me. It's a medium-sized orange book."

"A remarkable dramatist, if I may say so, sir."

"You admire him?"

"Exceedingly, sir."

"We must discuss *The Dutchess of Malfi* sometime."

"I would welcome such an opportunity."

Devlin went down the hall with the dog beside him. He was clearly impressed. "An amazing person, Iams," he said to the dog. "I always knew he thought a great deal of Fulke Greville, but this is something new."

They went in the bathroom to await the doctor's arrival.

TEN

The weather showed signs of clearing during the forenoon; by one o'clock the sun had come out. Its light, falling through an opening in the drapes on William's face, awakened him from a nightmare in which he searched, during a typhoon of Hollywood immensity, for a Grail which turned out to be an empty Coca-Cola bottle.

There were numerous vials and boxes of medicine on a table near the bed. It was a pleasant room with a log burning in the fireplace. From somewhere deep in the recesses of the house came a faint low booming, not unlike distant thunder.

Mrs. Shanahan at her kettledrums, he thought. He closed his eyes again and then quivered violently as he remembered his classes. It was several moments before it occurred to him that it was Saturday. Much relieved, he leaned on his elbow to watch, through the window, the leaves that fell from the maple trees.

Iams entered the room with breakfast on a tray.

"Good afternoon, sir. How are you feeling?"

"Better than I thought I would."

"Do you feel like eating a bit?"

"I'll try it."

Iams put the tray down. "I'll tell Mrs. Shanahan that you have awakened."

"Is Devlin up?"

"Mr. Devlin is still asleep, sir. He gave me explicit directions not to disturb him until the sun had set."

"Thank you, Iams."

"Is there anything else you wish?"

"No, this will be fine."

William was pleased to discover that he had an appetite. He had almost finished breakfast when Mrs. Shanahan paid him a visit. She was wearing a Russian blouse of heavy red silk and earrings with long pendants. There was an intense gleam in her eyes, brought on, had William but known, by her workout on the tympani. On two fingers of her outstretched right arm she carried a large and very disagreeable-looking parrot. She allowed it to perch on the back of a chair, where it looked at William with distinct irritation.

"How *are* you feeling this morning?" she inquired. "You poor boy, what a shame you had such a dreadful experience last night!" She sat on the bed and examined his face critically. "When Dorothy Bruce heard about what happened, she was awfully upset—you going to so much trouble and all. Say hello to Mr. Clay, Modigliani."

"Harya, big boy," the parrot croaked obediently.

"He's quite uncouth. Those pajamas you're wearing belonged to my first husband, Mr. Walpole. He was an Australian, you know, and in many ways my favorite husband. I've always kept those pajamas around for sentimental reasons, never dreaming they'd come in handy. How do they fit?"

"Very well. Perhaps you'd rather I didn't wear them."

"Of course not! They're very becoming. We can't have you convalescing in the raw."

"Did Dorothy—"

"I believe Mr. Walpole told me they were made in Belgium. That was years ago. Mr. Walpole was killed during a hunting trip in Nigeria, or did I tell you?"

"No."

"Shot in the back of his head by one of his own men. Frightful thing. Accidental, of course. The doctor says you must stay in bed for a while longer and drink a great deal of water." She worked with her hair to keep a large strand from falling over her forehead. "Stay where you are, Modie! It's really a shame you weren't around to go with us to see the airplane accident. Not a very good one, though. I've seen much better. No one was killed, although a lot of people were mashed up a good deal and it was rather awful in all that rain and mud. And then Melvin Lund and Dorothy had the most awful fight, and before that, Chester Thompson got in a quarrel with him and said a lot of unpleasant things. Melvin Lund had been telling us that he was thinking of taking a job that he'd been offered somewhere in the South, and Chester Thompson said, 'Our gain is their loss,' or something like that and they nearly came to blows. I rather like Melvin; of course, I've always been partial to Harvard men. Princeton, too, and Dartmouth. You didn't go to Dartmouth, did you?"

"No."

"Chester is crazy about Dorothy, you know. Tries to seduce her every chance he gets, I feel sure. He makes it so difficult for his wife, the poor thing; but I don't know, sometimes I think she likes the way he treats her, just asks for it. Of course men are always crazy about Dorothy. I suppose you are, yourself . . . Modigliani!"

"It's very kind of you to put me up, Mrs. Shanahan."

"Why, it's nothing at all! People are always staying here. You can see I love company. Why, Marcus Liebling, a musician I asked here for over the weekend, stayed with me for a whole year. Did you ever hear of him? Quietest, nicest man you ever saw, never made a bit of trouble, except once in a while he'd smoke a little opium in his room. But heavens, that happened so seldom no one minded at all, and he was always perfectly grand about playing his flute whenever anybody wanted him to. Which was not often, of course. Then one day he got a telegram and went away. Lovely person, although later we did miss some silverware."

"Does Dorothy Bruce— "

"Modie!" Mrs. Shanahan exclaimed. "Really! I'm afraid I must put you back in your cage if you are not good. Oh, I forgot to tell you, the Alpha Phis have had Mumford Bateson thrown in jail for stealing that *mammoth* dog of theirs. They've been bothering me continually on the telephone all morning. I saw the dog last night but it's certainly not around anyplace this morning. The fuss they've been making!"

"It's probably in Devlin's room."

"Oh, do you think so? Well, they'll just have to wait. I am certainly not going to bother Christopher for a bunch of silly girls." Mrs. Shanahan extended her fingers for the parrot to climb upon. "I was a Delta Gamma in my salad days," she told William.

In the doorway she paused and turned. "I nearly forgot to tell you," she said. "Dorothy thinks she left her bag last night and she'll be around this afternoon to see if she can find it. So you'll probably see her. You'll like that, won't you? Make yourself at home."

William spent the next three hours in a state of unprecedented exhilaration. He had not been so excited since his unsuccessful appearance before the committee delegated to select a Rhodes Scholar. It had all been worth it, he felt, more than worth it— the horrifying evening, the rain, the fever, the cold and greasy garage, the disappointment he had felt when she had not been there to drink the Coca-Colas. He thought of her coming into the room to sit beside him on the bed, her arms filled with flowers she had picked for him. Her eyes would never leave him for an instant. It would be an afternoon of confessions and avowals, one he would never forget. Even his invalidism seemed opportune.

At each sound of the telephone or doorbell he would smooth the covers, rearrange his pillow, comb his hair, and allow an expression of affability to take possession of his features. The minutes went by with even greater reluctance than they did in his most dreaded classes. At four, he rang for Iams.

"Will you see if Mrs. Shanahan has heard anything from Miss Bruce?"

"Mrs. Shanahan went out just after lunch, Mr. Clay."

"She didn't say when she'd be back?"

"No."

"What time is it?"

"About four, sir. Mr. Devlin is in the den if you wish to see him."

"I think I'll get up. I feel much better."

"Are you sure you ought to, sir?"

"I feel all right. Will you get my clothes?"

"I've been pressing them, sir. They came out quite well, although your necktie is somewhat disintegrated. However, one was left behind last night in one of the bedrooms; you might wear it. I'm sure no one would mind."

"Would you bring it, please?"

The necktie Iams brought was very much to William's liking. He might have selected it himself. When he was dressed he went downstairs to the den, where he found Devlin stretched out on the davenport eating an omelette and reading a large book called *Black Rapture: The Sex Life of the African Negro*, by Dr. Leopold Blumenthal.

"Hello," Devlin said. "How are you feeling?"

"Not bad."

"No ill effects, eh?"

"It's those cold capsules I've been taking, I guess."

"Have you ever read *Black Rapture*?"

"No."

"You ought to read it, Bill. Sounds a little like the year I taught at that girls' school in Alabama."

William sat down. The St. Bernard, who had been sleeping near the fire, got up and put his head in William's lap.

"Are you a dog lover?" Devlin asked.

"No." William looked at Devlin. He needed a shave and his color was very bad.

"Dorothy's coming this afternoon," William said.

"Who?"

"Dorothy Bruce. The girl with Lund."

"So what?"

"Nothing. She's just coming. She thinks she left her bag here."

"Just so she doesn't bring Lund along to help her look for it. Where is the article?"

"I don't know. Mrs. Shanahan said she thought she'd left it."

"Quite a good-looking gal. Fantastic, though, her associating with Lund. An election bet, perhaps. She sings, you know. Sang for us last night while you were gone. Not so good, I'm sorry to say."

"Really?" William said icily.

"Not bad, but on the other hand, definitely not anything to have a paroxysm over."

William pushed the dog away and stood up.

"My God, you aren't in love with her, are you?" Devlin said.

"Well, what's the matter with that?"

"Nothing at all. As a matter of fact, it sounds like the very thing." Devlin rubbed his index finger over his mustache. "Sorry, Bill," he said in a mollifying tone. "Her voice just didn't happen to appeal to me."

William went to the window and looked out. It was a clear autumn day, mild and windless, the sort of day on which one feels that somewhere, where one ought to be, things of moment are taking place. A block distant, on the highway, was a billboard with the words, "Tell Mummy Soft-Feel Tissue is Made of Fluff." There was a picture of a nurse delivering this tonic message to a pink-checked little girl, who seemed deeply moved.

"What time is it?" William said.

"I don't know. About four-thirty."

"Do you think she'll come?"

"I wouldn't be surprised."

William came away from the window and sat down beside Devlin. "Did she say anything about me last night?"

"Not that I recall."

"Do you think she likes Lund?"

"Jesus, Bill, how should I know? Why not ask her?"

The telephone rang and William jumped noticeably. He listened with an intent expression while Iams was talking in the hallway. He could hear nothing. When he had hung up, William called to him.

"That wasn't Miss Bruce, was it, Iams?"

"No sir."

"I just thought it might be."

"A young lady from the Alpha Phi sorority. They're sending over for their dog."

William leaned back and stared dreamily at the painting of Dorothy Bruce. "It doesn't do her justice," he said.

"What's that?"

"The painting."

"Oh, yes."

William did not feel that Devlin was displaying the proper amount of interest in the discussion. There were times when this attitude of Devlin's annoyed him. William stood up restlessly and looked out of the window.

"It is strange, her running around with Lund."

Devlin was reading the book again. "Um," he said.

"I wonder why she does."

"Maybe she goes in for collecting strange types. Thompson and Lund seem to support that theory."

William frowned and moved a chair closer to the window where he could look out. It was beginning to get dark. He was still sitting there some twenty minutes later, when the telephone rang again. He felt tense and unnerved as he listened to Iams talking.

"Well?" he said, looking up expectantly as Iams came into the room.

"That was Miss Bruce, sir. She found her purse. It was in Mr. Lund's topcoat pocket. Fortunate she found it, wasn't it?"

When neither of them made any comment, he asked, "Is there anything I can get for either of you?"

"I'd like a drink," Devlin said.

"Whiskey?"

"Whiskey."

"I think I'll go home," William said.

"Stick around," said Devlin. "Maybe there'll be some excitement this evening."

"I've got some things I ought to do."

"They can wait."

"I think I'd better run along."

"See you Monday, then."

"Thanks for taking care of me last night."

"Not at all."

William wrote a precise little note, thanking Mrs. Shanahan for her hospitality. Sometimes he had the feeling that social life was not for him. There were too many complications. He did not mention this in his note to Mrs. Shanahan.

As he went down the walk, a car filled with determined Alpha Phis drew up in front of the house. Recognizing one of his students, he walked faster.. He had eighty themes yet to correct, and there would be a letter from Frances asking him why he hadn't written. He did not like to think about Frances.. The Alpha Phi car roared by him. The St. Bernard was on the running board, held there by an ingenious arrangement of straps.

ELEVEN .

On the blackboard, in addition to his own writing, were many baffling diagrams chalked there during the previous hour by Dr. Fisher. William, for the life of him, could not see what possible connection they had with *The Ring and the Book*, yet Dr. Fisher no doubt knew what he was doing.

He sat at his desk for several moments looking at the diagrams. He was waiting until the last member of 101g had gone. Then he stepped down from the dais, erased the blackboard and wiped the chalk dust from his hands. He had done something he had never done before; something, in fact, that he had never contemplated doing. He had dismissed his class fifteen minutes early. It had been the only thing left to do, for he had sat there looking at his students for an interminable length of time, unable to think of anything to say. His mind had gone quite blank.

Going down the hall, he determined to take measures to make sure that such a thing never happened again. Maybe they figured he was sick, he thought. He fervently hoped that Dr. Showers would not learn what happened. It was the sort of thing Devlin was always getting into trouble about. It would be a different matter if he were an older member of the department or a well-established eccentric.

The door of the office next to his was open and,

inside, Dr. Funk and Mr. Calmer were discussing the event that had taken place on the campus the Tuesday before. Mr. Dunklee, a young member of the Physics Department, had chased one of his colleagues, Dr. Metcalfe, up and down the stairs of Mary Walburton Vitz Hall, screaming wildly at him and flourishing a revolver. When Dr. Metcalfe had dashed into a janitor's closet and locked the door behind him, Mr. Dunklee had shot four times through the door, hitting Metcalfe three times. Metcalfe had died at once. Mr. Dunklee thereupon proceeded to very messily commit suicide. There had not been such excitement on the campus since three years before, when the Dean of Women, an unmarried lady, had returned from the Orient, looking decidedly pregnant.

William went in the office and borrowed a match from Mr. Calmer.

"Dunklee was out of his mind," said Dr. Funk. He was sitting on his desk, cleaning his fingernails with a paper knife. He looked at William as though no one were there. "Think of Metcalfe's family. They say he carried no insurance at all."

"It's a shame, a shame," said Mr. Calmer. He found the topic wearisome, but continued to listen to Dr. Funk with respect since he was quite sure Dr. Funk would become head of the department if anything were to happen to Dr. Showers.

"Shot through the door, there in the dark. Dunklee

was insane. They were supposed to have been working together on a paper."

"I understand it was on thermo-elastic behavior of composite plates," said Mr. Calmer.

"Was that it?" said Dr. Funk with interest.

"The manuscript was nearing final form."

"Thank you for the match," William said, going out.

"I guess old Threlkeld will have to get a couple of new men," said Dr. Funk. He seemed not to have noticed William. "Pretty much of a blow to his department."

William went to his office. He had lost interest in the Metcalfe-Dunklee affair. No one talked of anything else these days. It was certainly having a great success. He picked up a mimeographed bulletin which had been left under the door, announcing the appointment of Eugene Orville Oates, B.S. (Commerce), '32, as Assistant Publicity Director of the University. William put it in the wastebasket and got his hat and topcoat.

He did not have to wait long for a streetcar. He rode downtown and got off with a thin colored woman who was carrying a rattan suitcase. It had "Boneless Corsets" printed on it. He walked two blocks to the Hotel Hubbard, slowing his pace to avoid walking directly behind the Negress. It was in the Hotel Hubbard, he had learned, that Dorothy Bruce worked.

The Tuesday following the party at Mrs. Shanahan's, he had gone to the Public Library and searched in the city directory for her name. The book was a year old and listed two Dorothy Bruces, one unidentified, and the other described as an employee of the Bluebird Laundry. When he had called at the address listed for the first, an apartment house not far from campus, he had been informed, by an old man who did not hear well, that Miss Bruce had moved a long time ago. By diligent effort, William eventually discovered that she worked at one of the town's three radio stations. The night before, he had listened to a program on which she sang. Devlin, he felt, had been greatly mistaken in his estimate of her voice.

The lobby of the hotel was crowded with men wearing purple ribbons on their lapels, and a sign above the elevator proclaimed a welcome to the dentists of the State. There was a large drawing of a tooth on an easel. William asked a bellboy, who was leaning against a pillar, where the studios were.

"You see those stairs over there?" the bellboy said, pointing to insure fixing their location in William's mind. "Well, bud, it's right up to the mezzanine and to your right."

William moved through the crowd and climbed the stairs, wondering, among this throng of dentists, if he should not have his teeth cleaned and scaled before long. It had been almost a year since they had been gone over.

There was a woman at a desk who looked up as he entered. She wore horn-rimmed glasses. A row of rooms with large plate-glass windows stretched on either side of her; and, from a loudspeaker by the receptionist's desk, a grim voice was delivering the weather report.

"I'd like to see Miss Bruce," William said. "Miss Dorothy Bruce."

"Would you?"

"Yes."

"She's in there," the woman said, nodding toward one of the studios. "She'll be out in a minute." William thanked her and sat down. The chair made a noise as his weight settled into it.

"You're not the man from Kewpie Kandies, are you?" the woman asked.

"No."

William lowered his eyes and contemplated the shine on his shoes. A man in his shirtsleeves came down the hall, perspiring freely and scanning a handful of papers with a busy air. He entered one of the studios. The voice on the loudspeaker, its grim inflections discarded, announced a quarter of an hour program of Hawaiian melodies.

While William listened to steel guitars, a pimply individual, resembling the young men in ointment advertisements, appeared in the doorway holding a trombone. "You haven't seen Gus, have you?" he called to the woman at the desk. "I don't think he's shown up yet," she said.

The program featuring Hawaiian melodies was well under way, and growing in volume, when Dorothy came out. She was wearing a gray suit and hat, and around her neck was a necklace of seashells.

"Hello," he said, getting up.

"Well, hello, what are you doing here?" She smiled brightly at him.

"I wanted to see you."

"Gee, I'm glad you came down. Why didn't you do it before? Why didn't you call me up?"

"I didn't know where you were."

He held the door open for her and they went down the stairs.

"Dentists" she said. "Did you ever see so many dentists? Last night one of them got drunk and fell off the rail around the mezzanine. Was there ever excitement! Gee, I'm glad you came around. Are you taking me to lunch?"

"Of course. That's why I came."

"You know, I sort of hoped you'd call me. You were so swell—going after a Coke for me in all that storm. Annabelle said you had an awful time."

"It was nothing."

"I was perfectly disgusted with Melvin. You knew I'd broken up with him, didn't you? Well, I have. Gee, he was perfectly impossible that night. He can be awful. Where do you want to go?"

"Wherever you'd like."

"There's a good place around the corner."

"Let's go there."

It was a chromium and red-leather place with fish swimming in a tank in the window.

"Look," she said, taking him by the arm. "I want you to see my fish."

William followed her to the tank. It was filled with goldfish. They moved with a peculiarly sluggish effort, as though they were feeling the effects of the water, which appeared not to have been changed of late.

"See that one!" she said, pointing at a speckled pink fish which was now floating languidly in the direction of a miniature stone castle, overgrown with moss. Her eyes grew large with a look of pleasure as she turned to him and exclaimed, "Isn't he swell! Gee, I think he's the swellest fish!"

"He is pretty nice," William said with as much warmth as he could.

"I don't think you really like him the way I do," she said.

"On the contrary."

"You couldn't begin to like them the way I do. Golly, I'd like to have a big place in the country with a pool, you know, a real clear one, just full of them. We used to have a pool like that when we lived in Palo Alto, when I was a little girl. I used to go out there and wade. Did you ever have a fish come up and nibble at your toes?"

"No."

"It's fun."

"I had an aunt who lived in Palo Alto."

"Did you?" She was looking at the fish again.

"She knew President Hoover slightly."

Now it was the vision of the child Dorothy that claimed him utterly, her skirts tucked up around her waist and the sun on her small legs, while tiny fish nibbled lovingly at her toes. Looking at her now, aware of the faint odor of her perfume, he was limp with the knowledge, the realization that she was with him. His heart pounded violently.

It was with reluctance that she left the tank. He walked behind her between the tables, watching her legs and hips and the way she carried her body.

"See those people over at that table, looking at us?" she said when they had been seated at a booth in the back corner. "They're all from the studio. They're trying to make out who you are."

"Who's the fat one?"

"Oh, that's Fred Robertson; he writes continuity. Have you ever heard the Mother Moomaw show?"

"No."

"He writes it. He's so funny! They're all pretty nice . . .Hello, Fred!" she called, waving to him. Still smiling, she examined the menu as the waitress came over to take their order.

"Do you like it there?" William asked when the

waitress had gone. "At the radio station?"

"Oh, it's swell! I've only been there a little while, but it's about as much fun as anything I've ever been in. There's always something happening around there, and talk about amazing people! See the girl sitting next to Fred Robertson? She just got a job in the East the other day. She plays swing on a harp!"

"What is it that you do?"

"Gee, I do everything under the sun. I sing and act and now I'm writing a little program. Don't think I wasn't glad to get that job! I was stranded here without a dime and I didn't know what I was going to do. Did you ever get stranded?"

"No."

"Don't ever. It's no fun. I don't know, I always get so *involved*. Do you get involved? It's funny how things work themselves out, isn't it?"

"What about your parents?"

"They're dead." As she looked up at him, it struck him suddenly that she was older than he had thought; there was something about her look at that moment, something in the expression around the eyes, that made him realize that she was not nineteen or twenty, but closer to his own age.

"They've been dead a long time," she said.

"I'm sorry," William said.

"Are *your* folks living?" she asked.

"Yes."

"My mother died when I was awfully small. Dad

always had a lot of money until the crash, and then I lived with some relatives in Los Angeles. Gee, they were pretty bad. They wouldn't let me do anything. I guess I was pretty wild then, though. I was fifteen and I wanted to get in the movies. And I did, too! I was in a couple of two-reelers, comedies with Charlie Chase and people like that. You know, you wouldn't believe it, but it was about the hardest work I ever did. I liked it, though. Gosh, did I have a crazy time! Then I got married. Sixteen years old and I didn't know what it was all about."

"Who was he?"

"An actor. He was crazy about me and I was crazy about him—for awhile. He'd just come to Hollywood and he wanted to do Shakespeare and we used to go down to the Bowl every night when nobody was there for a while—"

"The Bowl?"

"The Hollywood Bowl. You know, where they have all the concerts." She was not eating much and she asked William for a cigarette. "Carl and I used to go out there and I'd sit way up at the top in the back. The stars would be out and the moon and Carl would go up on the stage and do Othello and Hamlet and, you know, the king—"

"Lear."

"Yes. Gee, it's funny to think about all that now." She leaned back as he lit the cigarette for her. "It seems so awfully long ago. He had a wonderful voice. Really! Sometimes I wonder what's ever become of him. I thought I saw him in a mob scene once in a costume picture, but I never could be positive."

"How did you happen to break up?"

"Oh, he didn't treat me very well after a while. And then he hardly ever had any work and after a while I couldn't seem to get anything. We just about starved, and then I got a job at an orange-juice place in Long Beach. I wore a funny green outfit and hopped cars. Then Carl started running around with a girl who was a fashion designer in Santa Monica and—well, I left him about that time." She looked down at her hands. "Golly, it's funny the things people will do, isn't it?"

"Did you get a divorce?"

"Oh, yes. I didn't have any trouble."

William, stirring his coffee, felt touched. What a life she had had! he thought, seeing in himself the answer to all her problems—the person who always could be counted on, untainted by fickleness or a tendency to associate with fashion designers.

"Gee, why don't we go for a ride?" she said, smiling at him. "Let's go out in the country for a while. I don't have to be back until three."

William, somewhat unnerved, fumbled for a cigarette and avoided looking at her. "Well, I—"

"Oh, you've got a class!" she said, as he hesitated. "Is that it?"

"No. I'd cut it, if I did. My car's in the garage, getting worked over. What about tomorrow night, though?" he said. "It should be ready by then."

It would be ready, all right, he thought, planning rapidly. A withdrawal of the Ph. D. savings would be arranged. That would be more than enough for a down payment.

Walking back to the hotel, she took his arm. He stood at the bottom of the stairs and watched her as she left him.

"See you tomorrow night!" he called.

She turned and waved.

What legs! he could not help thinking. What marvelous eyes! The way she had smiled at him! He walked across the lobby, endeavoring to look stern and interesting.

At the cigar stand he bought a paper and looked through the used car ads. The dentists in the banquet hall were singing a song of fellowship. After a while he walked over to the bank and withdrew his savings. At three o'clock he drove back to Needham Hall in an only moderately used Ford roadster, black, with white sidewall tires and a conservative horn.

Melvin Cathcart Lund and a man from the Extension Division were standing in the hall discussing the Dunklee-Metcalfe affair when he came in. Melvin Cathcart Lund looked at William and did not speak. William smiled witheringly at him.

"The Physics Department has always been a hot

bed of jealousy," the man from the Extension Division was saying as William passed them to go to his office.

T W E L V E

It turned cold the next day. As he came down the steps of the Esterlings' house that evening, a sharp wind was blowing dead leaves down the street. He started the car and drove to the address Dorothy had given him. He was in a mellow and contented mood.

Going up the walk, he rang the bell, which tinkled with feeble effort in the distance. While he waited to be admitted, he dwelt on his plans for the evening. They would drive out to a fashionable roadhouse of which he had heard. He felt that this would please her. It was unlikely that Melvin Cathcart Lund had ever taken her there. He was certain that Lund was a cheapskate, for he had that look about him. William pictured Dorothy and himself dancing, the most attractive couple on the floor. He pushed the bell again.

A slatternly woman in a soiled wrapper and red felt carpet slippers let him in. She had an empty milk bottle in her hand and brushed by him to deposit

it on the porch. As the door opened, the odor of
cheap incense hit him in the face. The hallway was
illuminated by a globe that furnished the absolute
minimum of light. By squinting a bit, he found the
number of Dorothy's apartment listed on the directory and went up the stairs to the third floor. Somewhere in the building someone was playing, or
attempting to play, a series of notes on a saxophone.
A small child provided a counterpoint of fierce screams.
At the door he knocked and waited, glancing around
a trifle nervously.

"Were you looking for Dorothy?" a girl's voice
behind him said.

Standing in the doorway opposite was an extremely
tall but very well-proportioned girl wearing a dress
made from numerous red bandanna handkerchiefs.
She had long black hair with ragged bangs. Tower-
ing over him, she inspected him with interest.

"Dorothy had to go down to the station about
something. She told me to tell you." She stared at
him as though trying to reconcile his actual appearance with some earlier conception. "You *are* Mr.
Clay, aren't you?"

"Yes."

"I'm Ingrid Spitalnick."

"How do you do?" said William

"Are you a writer?" she asked.

"No. A teacher."

"I knew *that*. I thought maybe you wrote, too.

Many teachers are frustrated writers. I write proletarian short stories."

"Do you?"

"I just finished one today," she confided. "It's
about a scab."

Two doors down, a dark little man with rat-like
eyes looked at them.

"Who was that?" William said, as the man pulled
in his head and closed the door.

"Oh, that's Mr. Paulino," she said. "We think he
sells marijuana to high school students. Are you
interested in proletarian literature?"

"I don't know very much about it," William said.

"Miss Spitalnick!" a voice called from somewhere
below. "Telephone!"

"Well, goodnight, Miss Spitalnick," William said.

"Goodnight! See you again!"

He drove to the hotel, experiencing some difficulty in finding a place to park nearby, for the dentists'
convention was now in full swing. He called Dorothy
from a telephone in the lobby.

"Gee, I'm terribly sorry about this, but it just couldn't
be helped," she said. "It looks like I may have to
be here for an awful long time; so if you want to
call the date off, why, it'll be all right." She seemed
out of breath. Someone in the studio with her was
emitting strange animal cries, and a piano was being
played.

"I wouldn't think of it. How long will you be?"

He waited while she talked to someone about this. After a while she said, "I don't think over an hour. Gosh, wouldn't it make you sore, though?"

"I'll wait for you in the lobby."

"All right, darling," she said, hanging up.

Darling! He sat for a moment with the receiver still in his hand, staring with a moist look at the sign on which directions for the use of the telephone were printed. It was not until he began to notice how bad the air in the booth had become that he replaced the receiver and went down the steps to the bar in the basement to have a double scotch.

It was a very dark bar. William could scarcely see himself in the mirror. He sat on a high stool and ate potato chips. Although the booths were well filled, the only other person at the bar was a prematurely gray-haired man wearing a Basque shirt.

"Always drink scotch, do you?" he said to William.

"Not always."

"I prefer rye." He tapped his fingernail against his own glass. "You were certainly fried to the ears at Ethel's the other evening, I must say. Do you always run around with that little kleptomaniac?"

"I think you must have me confused with someone else," William said with dignity.

A woman with a tambourine dressed in a Salvation Army uniform came in selling the *War Cry*. William bought a copy but the man in the Basque shirt did not. He had an alert expression like that of one who has been served frequently with summonses.

"You must have been stinking," he said to William when the Salvation Army woman had gone. "Don't even remember it, eh? What about your telling Alfred and me about your girl in Indianapolis and the way she was tattooed and then passing out in the bathroom?"

"What do I owe you?" William said to the bartender.

"Thirty-five."

After a while the man in the Basque shirt wandered over to the jukebox and William went back upstairs. He sat in the lobby and watched the dentists. A man wearing dark glasses sat down beside him and began to eat peanut brittle. After a while, having emptied his sack, he went away.

William tried to read the *War Cry*. The thought struck him that he was getting nowhere with his Crashaw article. He took a piece of paper from his pocket, a laundry list, and wrote: "It is with Crashaw's great poem *A Hymn to the Name and Honor of the Admirable Saint Teresa* that I am here concerned. Professor Ellery Crouch, in his admirable study of Crashaw, has pointed out . . . "

He stopped writing and stared at what he had

written. But what was it that Professor Ellery Crouch had pointed out? he wondered. If he had ever known, he was unable to say now what it might be. And why "admirable"? Thinking back on the article, it impressed him now as dull and labored in the extreme. He struck out "admirable." Or perhaps the lobby of the Hotel Hubbard was simply not the place for this sort of thing, he reflected.

He wondered if something was happening to him. He had never felt quite this way before. Disturbed, he put the paper back in his pocket and looked at the clock. It was ten-thirty. He had been waiting for almost two hours.

When Dorothy appeared, wearing a black formal gown, she could not apologize enough. "I bet you could murder me," she said.

"I didn't mind at all," he said. "The time passed very quickly."

"Gosh, sometimes they think you don't have any private life at all, I guess," she said. "I thought you'd be mad at me."

They went out to the car and got in. She had never looked so beautiful to William. There was no one on the street, no one to see. He put his arm around her and attempted to kiss her.

"No."

"Why not?"

"No."

He pulled her over to him and kissed her hard.

He made it last as long as he could. Half way through it, she put her arms around his neck.

"Why did you say not to?" he said in her ear.

"I don't know."

"Didn't you want me to?"

"Yes."

"Then why did you say not to?"

"Gee, you ask a lot of questions, don't you?"

He kissed her again.

"You'd better not, anymore," she said. "It's pretty public here."

"I don't care."

"Please don't do that." She changed the position of the rear-vision mirror and fixed her hair and put on lipstick. "Bill?"

"Yes."

"What do you say we go over to the Thompsons'? They're having a party and they want us to come."

"I don't think they want *me* to come."

"Oh yes they do."

"Wouldn't you rather go someplace and dance? I thought we'd go out—"

"Gee, I'm too tired to dance. We'll have fun over there at Chester's."

"Will we?"

"Sure we will. They always have marvelous parties. I love to go there." She squeezed his hand. "Gee, don't you want to go?"

He shifted gears and backed out.

"You're not mad, are you?" she asked.
"No."
"I wouldn't want you to be mad."
"Which way do we go?" he said.

Chester Thompson and his wife lived in an apartment on the top floor of an otherwise abandoned building on the outskirts of the city. It was in a gloomy and desolate region. Real estate speculators had enchanted themselves into the erroneous and groundless belief that it might one day develop into a neighborhood distinguished for its smartness and high rents but, largely because of the construction of a tannery nearby and the frequent disposition of the wind to blow precisely in the wrong direction, nothing had come of these plans. Block after block of streets had been laid out and tall weeds grew around the white signs that marked the names of the streets, which honored American naval heroes. The ground floor of the building in which the Thompsons lived had previously served as an office for the real estate men and, during a later and gayer period, as the branch storehouse of some Italians from Chicago who specialized, during the 'twenties, in a brand of rye known as "Happy Valley."

The apartment cost the Thompsons fifteen dollars a month, a sum modest enough to permit Chester Thompson to run up a larger liquor bill than other wise would have been possible. He was also attracted by the sound of their address: One Dewey Drive, and the view of the city lights at night.

Although it was not actually late, the party, everyone agreed, was off to a good start by the time William and Dorothy arrived. One of the out-of-town guests, a raffish-looking man with a goatee who had been brought by Marvin Herendeen, had attempted to seduce one of the local Lesbians, with discouraging results; Chester Thompson had quarreled with another guest over Degas and he had departed in considerable temper; and someone with a cigar had burned a hole in one of Mrs. Thompson's prized tapestries. It was like many previous evenings at the Thompsons'.

A number of the same people who had been at Mrs. Shanahan's party were in evidence, but there were many others whom William had never seen before.

"Gee, don't you like this place!" Dorothy said.

Before he was able to phrase a reply, she had vanished to leave her coat in one of the other rooms, and he found himself confronted by Mrs. Thompson, who was offering him a glass of some yellowish liquid.

"I'm so glad you could come," she said. "Do you know all these people?"

"Most of them," he said. He noticed that since he had last seen Mrs. Thompson, she had acquired a black eye, which she had attempted to conceal with cosmetics, though none too successfully.

"Just make yourself at home," she told him, handing him the glass as someone called to her.

Alone, he sat gingerly on a bench and inspected the room, a barn-like affair hung with Chester Thompson's paintings. Representing the work of ten years, each painting documented the momentary enthusiasms by which the painter had at one time or another been seized. There were imitations of the Flemish school, primitive art, a portrait in the manner of some particularly unskilled R.A., a farm scene dominated by a bony and undernourished cow, three "Picassos"—one from the Blue Period, one *collage*, one example of Cubism—and what appeared to be an attempt to beat Wassily Kandinsky at his own game. William, though genuinely moved by this display of eclecticism, felt that none of them quite came up to his portrait of Dorothy.

He was thinking of the portrait when he became aware of a girl sitting beside him on the bench. She wore a dirty powder-blue sweater and her complexion was not good.

"I don't remember ever seeing you here before," she said.

"This is my first time."

"Do you paint?" she asked.

"No, I'm afraid not."

"You're not the one they call Mordecai Boepple, are you?"

"No. Who is he?"

"I don't know. I just thought you might be him."

"Is he a painter?"

"I don't think so. No, I'm quite sure he isn't. You don't mind my saying that you have the hands of a painter, do you?"

"Not in the least. Do you think I have?"

"That's what made me ask you."

Someone wound a portable phonograph and Bing Crosby sang *At Your Command*. It was a very old, cracked record.

"I loathe Bing Crosby," the girl said.

"Do you?"

"I loathe him." She looked up at William with large eyes and suddenly began to weep. "Oh God, I've had such a hell of a life. You don't know what I've been through. Just hell, that's what it's been." She rubbed her face with the back of a very soiled hand and asked for a handkerchief.

William gave her the one from his breast pocket. She blew her nose with vigor and returned it to him.

"You look like the sort of person that would understand," she said. "First it was my father. A bastard if there ever was one. He stood there and tore up my scholarship and laughed at me. I will never forget it, never! He was one of those bastards you want to kill. Oh, you couldn't possibly realize what it was like for me, standing there watching him tear it up and drop the pieces over the banister."

Dorothy had come out of the bedroom and was now talking to the young man who had been playing piano at Mrs. Shanahan's. He had brought an accordion with him this evening. Dorothy was smiling up at him, talking animatedly and gesturing with one arm.

"You don't know what it's been like for me!" the girl was saying. "It's been hell, that's what it's been, absolute hell. Aren't you going to drink your drink? Give it to me if you aren't."

"Help yourself," William said, handing her the glass. "Please excuse me for a moment. I think I see someone I know."

Catching sight of Devlin in a corner of the room, inspecting one of his host's paintings, William hurried over to him.

The painting was one William had missed. It represented, among other things, melting telephone poles and a huge bloodshot eye which, floating in space, was losing its lashes. There was also a vast expanse of sand and what might well have been a disembodied navel.

"Didn't expect to see you here," Devlin said.

"I didn't expect to be here myself."

"But Dorothy insisted."

"Yes."

"Not often, but once in a while, I get the drift." Devlin raised the glass he was holding and drank what was left in it. He made a face and shuddered. "Good God!" he exclaimed. "This stuff the Thompsons serve puts me in mind of a drink described to me by a bird I knew who once lived in Hawaii. Seems the Hawaiian proletariat mix up a barrelful of rice, decayed pineapple, coconut, and then toss in a plug of chewing tobacco, just for good measure. When this mess ferments, they throw a party."

In the middle of the room, surrounded by an admiring crowd, one of the guests was giving a very realistic demonstration of an epileptic fit.

"That's Al Merton," Devlin explained, as they watched him roll on the floor. "He always does his epileptic fit act at parties."

"Always?"

"I've never seen a time that it hasn't been splendidly received."

"He even froths," William observed.

"Soap flakes," said Devlin. "He carries them around in his pocket."

They moved closer to get a better view.

"What set him off tonight?" Devlin asked Marvin Herendeen, who was standing nearby, inserting a cigarette in a holder.

"Oh, Al was telling Chester that he was one guy they'd never take if we had another war, and that little lez with Virginia asked him why not. So he had to demonstrate, naturally."

"Naturally," said Devlin.

Bing Crosby sang *Shine On, Harvest Moon* until the motor ran down.

"Not that he'll ever have to make use of it," Marvin Herendeen said. "I don't think there's the slightest chance we'll ever mess in Europe again."

"Don't you?" said Devlin.

"We learned our lesson last time."

"Um."

"You don't agree?"

"It's an interesting point of view."

"You don't agree."

"No."

"Why should we become involved?"

Devlin looked around the room and said, "Where can I get some more of this stuff?"

"I say, why should we become involved?" Herendeen persisted.

"Because something will be in jeopardy."

"What?"

"I don't know. Something."

Dorothy was still talking to the pianist.

"The American people will never stand for it," said Herendeen.

"Perhaps not," Devlin said. "Right now I need a drink."

William said, "I had one, but that girl took it."

"What girl?"

"I don't know. She had hysterics and started on a crying jag."

"Oh, don't pay any attention to her. Did she tell you about her father tearing up her scholarship?"

"Yes."

"She always works him in," said Devlin.

"I asked her once what school it was for," Herendeen said. "My recollection is that it was one of those chiropractic places."

They left Herendeen since his height made conversation difficult for any length of time. The room was growing more and more noisy. Al Merton was rinsing the soap from his mouth and Chester Thompson was complimenting him on the new effects he had recently added to his act. Nelson Castleman was telling a tall blonde girl with a bulging forehead about his collection of books on taxidermy. Someone had found a comparatively new needle for the phonograph and it was now playing an old Jean Goldkette recording which was much admired because of the belief that Bix Beiderbecke took a chorus on it, although this was an unconfirmed rumor, and totally without foundation. A little group in one corner of the room was quietly denouncing Chester Thompson.

William looked around for Dorothy. She was dancing with the pianist.

William got another drink and stood watching her with the guarded smile of one who is never sure of his popularity. She danced very close to her companion, her eyes closed and her head drooping slightly to one side in such a way that her hair fell over one shoulder. Her back was bare and very white and smooth except for a small brown mole near her right shoulder blade.

They danced through four records before William approached her.

"Oh, there you are, Bill!" she said. Her eyes were bright and she was slightly flushed. Gee, I thought you'd gone off and deserted me."

"I was right over there."

"Were you? Gee, I didn't see you. You must have been hiding in back of something."

"No."

"I didn't see you *anywhere.*"

"You know, you dance marvelously."

"Do you really think so?"

"Marvelously."

Someone put on another record. On the other side of the room he could see Chester Thompson and his wife engaged in a quarrel.

"Dance this one with me?" William said.

She fanned herself with her hand. "Oh, gosh, not right away. I'm kind of tired. I wonder if they've got a Coca-Cola for me."

They had one. William sat with her on a couch while she drank it, and told her about gradations in faculty rank. He was surprised to learn that she was poorly informed along such lines.

"I only went to college for six weeks and then I

got fed up with it," she said. "They tried to make me take a whole lot of stuff I didn't want to take, like chemistry and mathematics. I'm not sorry I dropped out."

"You should have gone on." Looking around the room, he said, "Do you really like this, Dorothy?"

"What do you mean?"

"This party."

"Why, sure. Gee, I guess you ought to drink some more or something. Someone said the drinks are especially good tonight. You know, I don't drink because I just go crazy. Honest, one drink just makes me go wild."

, Next to them, a group was following up the earlier discussion on avoiding the draft.

"I'll tell them I'm a bed wetter," one man said. "The army is very quick to reject bed wetters."

"Having a good time?" Chester Thompson said, coming up. He appeared to be in an unusually expansive and genial mood. Sitting down between then, which he managed with skill, he said, "What do you think of our place? One Dewey Drive—how do you like the sound of it? You know, Dorothy, I got started painting again the other day and I feel like a million. Felt so good one day I took a sock at Doris. You saw her black eye, didn't you? Quite a poke I gave her." He looked at William. "Say, my friend, you need another drink. Go over and get yourself one. God knows there's enough tonight for everybody."

"I—"

"Go ahead! Don't be backward!"

The liquor was in a five-gallon crock in the kitchen. The table was littered with skins of oranges and lemons. Some had fallen off and been stepped on. Bessie Llewelyn was sitting on the floor telling a man with a birthmark about her father tearing up her scholarship. The man with the birthmark had closed his eyes and gave every evidence of having passed out. This did not deter Bessie Llewelyn.

When William came back, Dorothy was dancing with Chester Thompson. William pressed his lips together. He stood by the Kandinsky imitation, music and talk crashing around him. Keeping him waiting for hours and then saying she was too tired to dance. It certainly looked like she was too tired to dance, didn't it? Yet he knew, following her with his eyes, that she could treat him in any way she pleased, she could do anything she wanted, and he would still be hanging around, unprotesting. He did not like this knowledge, but there it was.

"May I cut?"

"Oh, there you are, Bill!"

"What's the idea, exactly?" he said when he had his arm around Dorothy and Chester Thompson had walked away in a bad humor.

"Gosh, I don't have any idea what you're talking about."

"Don't you?"

"No, I don't."

"You don't, eh?"

"You must have had a drink, all right."

"I had three. Very large."

"Gee, I think it's nice that you're tight. I like it when you're tight."

William said, "Look here, I asked you to dance with me and you said you were too tired, and just as soon as I left you, you started dancing with that bastard."

"What a thing to say! Gee, I would have danced with you, only, gosh, there for a minute I was tired. I don't see why you have to get mad about it."

The pressure of her body against his and the odor of her perfume mollified him a little.

"As a matter of fact," she went on, "he's going to give me painting lessons."

"Thompson?"

"Uh-huh. Ingrid Spitalnick and me. I've always wanted to paint and Chester thinks I have talent."

He did not know exactly what it was she was saying. He found, as their dance ended, that the three drinks had worked a curious effect on him. He had trouble focusing his eyes and an intense roaring had begun in his left ear. Back of his nose, someone seemed to be inflating a balloon. He walked over and leaned against the wall, feeling suddenly dizzy and faint, and attempted to steady himself.

"Do you feel all right, Bill?" Dorothy asked.

"Fine. I feel fine."

"You don't look it."

"I'm all right."

"Why don't you go in the bedroom and lie down for a while? Your color is simply awful."

He put one hand to his head and swayed slightly. Her face seemed to be enlarged. Back of her, the whole room swam, Chester Thompson's pictures moved up and down on the walls, and in his stomach a gruesome churning began. Devlin's description of the Hawaiian concoction rose in his mind, and he had a vivid picture of the natives at work around the barrel.

He staggered to the bedroom. A rumpled-looking man and woman came out at his approach and he went inside and stretched out on the bed. It immediately began to weave. He opened his eyes and stared at the ceiling to steady it. He had the feeling that the whole room was about to turn upside down. He could not understand why he had ever allowed her to talk him into coming here in the first place.

After a while he felt better and then much worse. Chester Thompson came in and sat down beside him.

"Not so good, eh?" he said.

"Not so good."

"Something you ate, maybe."

"Something I ate. That must be it."

"You didn't know Gus Coombs, did you?"

"No."

"This evening sort of makes me think of the party we had here last Christmas Eve. Same sort of quality. It was around midnight that Harry Quaintance remembered that he'd forgotten to get a Christmas present for his wife. She was at home, see, didn't come to the party with Harry because she doesn't like me. Are you listening?"

"She wouldn't come to the party, eh?"

"So Harry and I went downtown and he bought a waffle iron for his wife's Christmas present and got a turkey for dinner the next day and we went up to his place. This was around midnight, see? His wife was waiting for him in the hall when we came up yelling 'Merry Christmas!' Jesus, she always did have a temper, but was she sore that night! She came out on the porch and threw the waffle iron at him and hit me over the head with the turkey."

"What about Gus Coombs?"

"Gus? Oh, she ran off with Gus shortly after New Year's. I think they're living in the South. How you feeling?"

"Not so good."

"You wouldn't mind if I took Dorothy for a ride in your car, would you?"

"Yes, I would, rather." He rolled over and frowned at Chester Thompson. "Wouldn't oblige me by just loaning me your car for a little while, eh?"

"No."

"Okay," said Thompson, getting up. "Okay, if that's the way you feel about it." He was very pale.

William watched the door close behind him. He felt like a character in a magazine advertisement— one of those men who portray sufferers from "jangled nerves" or "acid indigestion," from whose heads lines radiate to suggest a throbbing pain. Where was Richard Crashaw now and where were the splendid classes and the brilliant students? Where were the fine, stimulating talks with his colleagues? The moonlight, sour and blue, hung like a reproach behind the curtains. He closed his eyes as the bed lurched horribly.

He felt as though he had slept the clock around when he was awakened by the sounds of struggle. Two men were thrashing about on the floor. His head was clearer now and gradually it became apparent to him that the men on the floor were Devlin and Chester Thompson. Both were breathing heavily and appeared to have arrived at a stalemate. Then suddenly Devlin jerked loose and hit Thompson so hard that he fell and struck his head on the floor.

Devlin went over and looked down at him. Then he straightened up and came over to William, adjusting his tie and rubbing the back of his neck.

"Are you all there?" he said to William.

"What the devil's going on?" William said. He sat on the edge of the bed, his hair mussed and a dreadful taste in his mouth.

Devlin picked up a butcher knife that was lying nearby.

"What's that?" William said.

"Chester came in here with this thing, a very intent look on his face. Evidently had the idea he wanted to cut you up. How do you feel?"

"Not bad."

"What got into him?"

"I told him he couldn't borrow my car. To take Dorothy for a ride."

"You'd better get out of here." Devlin put the knife under a magazine on the dresser.

"Damned lucky you happened to see him," said William.

"Yes, wasn't it?"

William combed his hair and they went into the other room. Everyone was very drunk by this time. Marvin Herendeen, scarcely able to see, staggered up to William and asked him if he had seen Mordecai Boepple. Two phonograph records had been broken and Nelson Castleman was complaining that his pocket had been picked. Bits of food were scattered about the room. A very drunk man wearing a lei was endeavoring to play the accordion. A group by the window was gravely discussing the prostate gland. It was discovered that someone had poured a drink into the interior of the phonograph. Bessie Llewelyn was stretched out, face down, in one corner. A good many of the guests had gone home.

William found Dorothy sitting on the stairs talking to a young man with a receding chin.

"Do you mind leaving now?" William said to her.

"What for? It's only one o'clock."

"It's really rather important."

"What's so important about it?"

"Say, you can't take Dorothy away yet," the young
man with the receding chin said.

"Come on, Dorothy," said William, taking her by
the arm.

"Gee, whatever is the rush, anyway?"

It did not seem right to blurt out that Chester
Thompson had tried to stab him. In the end, it took
a good deal of talking and she was noticeably irritable as they went down the steps. Devlin was standing
out in front, scraping some foreign matter from the
fender of his automobile.

"What's the matter, anyway?" Dorothy said. "What
are you looking so pale about? And stop pinching
my arm!"

"Thompson tried to take a knife to me while I
was asleep," William said.

"What! Oh, Bill, I simply don't believe it! What
did you say to him? What were you fighting about?"

"I didn't say anything to him. I didn't even see
him."

"I never heard of anything so fantastic. Why would
he want to do such a thing?"

"I have absolutely no idea."

"When did all this happen?"

"Just now. Ask Devlin. He'll tell you."

"It's a fact," Devlin said, scraping away the last particles of the foreign substance. "He went after him with a butcher knife. A very large butcher knife."

"You must be making it up," Dorothy said incredulously. "Why would Chester want to do a thing like that?"

Devlin said, "Didn't you ever hear about the time he tried to stab Annabelle Shanahan's butler? Or the time he went after Gus Coombs with a can opener?"

"I never heard of such a thing," Dorothy said. "I just can't make myself believe he'd do such a thing."

They discussed it at length but got nowhere and after a while Devlin said goodnight. It was cold outside. They watched him get in his car and put on his gloves. Someone opened a window above them and threw a victrola record a great distance. It struck a tree across the road and broke. There was much laughter.

"What's he sore about?" Dorothy said.

"He isn't sore."

"He certainly acted like it."

"Come on, let's get in the car," William said.

Someone had been ill on the running board. When they were inside, he started the engine and turned on the heater, but the air that came out was cold. He switched it off and they drove back to town in silence. Dorothy sat huddled up in the corner, away from him.

"I don't know why you're sore at *me*," William said. "But frankly, I didn't much want to stay around there and invite more trouble."

She didn't say anything.

"What's the matter?" he said. "Can't you talk to me?"

"I don't know what reason you have for making up stories like that about Chester, Bill. I've heard all kinds of things about him, but I just can't bring myself to believe them. Chester has always been perfectly wonderful to me. You must have been pretty drunk or you'd never have thought of such a thing."

"My God, he had a butcher knife a foot long. Why should I make up a thing like that? If it hadn't been for Devlin, I wouldn't be here now."

"The whole thing sounds perfectly fantastic."

He was tired of the whole affair. They had arrived at her apartment house. He switched off the lights.

"Dorothy," he said, taking hold of one of her hands. "Please don't be unreasonable with me. What I'm telling you is the God's truth."

She was looking out of the window. Her hand was limp and rather cold. When he tried to kiss her, she turned her head away so that his lips struck the vicinity of her ear.

"Please *don't!*" she said.

"Dorothy. Listen—"

"You're hurting my arm."

It was a dingy leave-taking. He drove back to the Esterlings and found a hysterical telegram from Frances. It contained exactly fifty words and was full of reproaches and vague threats. He tore it into small bits. Carrying them down to the bathroom through the dark hallway, he almost broke his neck when he tripped over the vacuum cleaner, which had fallen out of a closet. After he had limped into the bathroom, he discovered that someone had used the last of his toothpaste. Several cats howled under his window so that he had difficulty in getting to sleep.

T H I R T E E N

It was on the following Wednesday, late in the afternoon, that Dorothy called him. The weather had been almost warm and William had stayed late in his office, putting off the lonely and unattractive meal he would eat by himself in one of the less dismal campus restaurants. Following a heavy day of conferences, he was reading some test papers in which the 101g's had quite outdone themselves in missing the point. He looked up from a paper covered with fingerprints and switched on the light before he answered the telephone.

"Bill, are you terribly busy?"

She sounded disturbed. He was astonished to hear her voice. He said, "No, not awfully." It would not do to display too much warmth, he felt, considering the circumstances.

"Gee, I hated to bother you, but you're about the only person I could think of who has a car and might be able to get away . . . Hello?"

The connection was not good.

"Hello!" she said again. "Can you hear me? I don't know what's the matter with this phone. Listen, Bill, can you come out here and get me? I'm sort of in trouble."

"Where are you?"

"Out on Highway Nineteen, I think it is. Wait a minute. Wait just a minute." He could hear her talking to someone. After a while she said, "It's about four miles from the edge of town on the road to the Turnpike. It's painted orange. You won't have any trouble finding it."

"What's painted orange?"

"This filling station. Didn't I tell you I was at a filling station?"

"All right. I'll come right away."

"It's called 'Harold's'."

In the hallway he encountered Dr. Buckman, the retired Greek professor, who was rearranging his underclothing in the semi-darkness. He and Dr. Buckman did not speak. The streetlights came on as William went out to his car. The sky still held the fading colors of the sunset. He kept within the speed limit until he reached the edge of town; then he drove as though taking part in a moving-picture rescue. For three days he had fought off a painfully intense compulsion to call her, and he knew all too well that he would have given in that evening had she not called him first. He permitted himself to smile, slowing down as he neared the filling station. It would not do to appear too eager. His revenge might come in infinitesimal amounts, but he wanted a little of it.

In the twilight he could see Dorothy playing with a puppy in front of the place. She was wearing a gray sweater and a gray skirt, her head bare. Inside, an old man in coveralls was eating canned beans from a paper plate.

If she was not glad to see him, she gave a sufficiently good imitation of it. Running up to the car, the puppy after her, she seemed to William more like the girl he had first seen at the hotel bar.

"Am I ever glad to see you!" she said, as he held the car door open for her. The puppy attempted to climb in after her and she said, "No, no, Dinty!" She turned to William. "Isn't he the sweetest puppy?"

Harold was standing in the doorway holding the paper plate, which was now rather soggy. He watched them with a perplexed and not entirely approving expression as William turned the car around. Some of the tomato sauce from the beans had run down the front of his coveralls.

"Am I ever glad to see you!" she said again, pressing William's hand and looking up at him. "Give me a cigarette, will you? Gee, I'm simply starved. You don't happen to have any old chicken salad sandwiches hidden in the car, do you?"

"The other owner took them all, if there were any. Wouldn't Harold give you any of his beans?"

"They didn't look very good."

"What are you doing out here?" William said. Not too directly, he glanced at her.

"Oh gosh, I just hate to tell you about it. I always get so *involved*."

"What was it?"

"Well, you've heard of Baxter, haven't you?"

"No, I can't say that I have."

"Baxter the Great?"

"No."

"Well, he just came here last week. He's a mind reader at the station. He does a show twice a day for Munchy Muffins."

"For what?"

"Munchy Muffins. They're really very good."

"I see."

"It makes me mad every time I think of him. Gosh, he is the best-looking thing, though."

"Is he?"

"Gee, he's terribly attractive. About thirty-five, getting gray at the temples. Very dark with beautiful white teeth."

"A Negro?"

"You don't think I'd have anything to do with a Negro, do you?"

"Did you have something to do with Baxter?"

"Oh gosh," she said. "We were both leaving the hotel this afternoon at the same time and he asked me if he could take me home. So I said yes, if he wanted to. Well, we rode around for a while, and pretty soon he said that a friend of his had this cabin out in the country and he had to drive out there to see him about something and would I like to ride along. He said he'd just be a few minutes."

He waited.

"Well, we got out to this cabin and went up and knocked at the door and nobody answered, so Grant— that's his first name, Grant—tried the knob and the door was open. 'You might as well see the place, as long as you're out here,' he said. So I didn't think anything about it particularly and we went inside.

"Well, I'd noticed that he'd been acting kind of nervous and strange, and when we got inside he excused himself the very first thing and went in another room. I didn't think much about it one way or another, but he was gone such a long time I got sort of frightened. Well, I heard the funniest sound outside and I went out to see what it was. I never did find out, but when I went by one of the windows I looked in

and there he was in the bedroom, with his coat off
and his sleeves rolled up, sticking himself in the
arm with a hypodermic needle.

"I thought that was kind of funny and then I got
scared because once when I was in Hollywood an
extra who was a dope fiend tried to rape me, and it
was the awfullest experience I about ever had."

"He didn't succeed, did he?" William said.

"Oh no, I hit him over the head with a vase."

"What did you do? About Baxter?"

"Well, just as I looked in, he looked up and saw
me. He just stopped dead still, as though he was
paralyzed. I guess I did, too. The first thing I thought
of was to run for his car, and then I remembered
that he'd taken the keys out and put them in his
pocket. So I started running toward the road and I
fell down and tore my stocking." She lifted her dress,
exposing a rip at the knee. "Well, there was a farmer
with some cows, an awfully nice man, and I walked
along with him, and when I looked back, Grant was
standing a little way off the road, looking as though
he were out of breath."

"And then you called me from Harold's?"

"Didn't I tell you I get involved? Gee, what do
you suppose he'll say when I see him at the studio
tomorrow?

They were approaching the edge of town. "I'll
tell you what!" Dorothy said. "Let's stop at this
grocery store up here and get some things for a picnic."

"Would you like that?"

"Gee, it's so nice out. I think it would be fun."

He stopped the car and they went inside and bought wieners and butter and buns, a jar of olives, apples, and a bottle of red wine.

"I know a swell place where we can go," Dorothy told him.

To get there, they had to drive back for several miles and then turn off on a country road. After a while she told him to turn again and presently they came to the place. He parked the car away from the road and locked the doors. Prepared for a rudimentary emergency such as this, William produced an old blanket from the trunk in back. By the light of his flashlight, which blinked as though it might go out at any moment, they crawled under a barbed-wire fence and walked down a hill.

There was a grassy stretch of ground under a tree by a creek. William lowered the wine bottle into the cold water at the stream's edge and came back to help her spread out the blanket. The dry leaves cracked under their feet as they picked up wood for a fire. There were many stars out. A mile distant, on the highway, they could see the headlights of speeding cars, and beyond that, the pearl-gray glow of lights from the town.

"I just feel awful about the other night," Dorothy said.

"Forget it."

"Oh, gosh, when Chester admitted what he'd done,
I just felt horrible. But you understand what's wrong
with him, why, it's really very simple."

"What *is* wrong with him?"

"He has these urges."

"I see."

"Urges he can't resist at all. Gosh, you don't know
what it's like for him, Bill! He's just like he was in
a trance! And after it's over he can hardly remember anything that went on or anything he did."

"After what's over?"

"These comas he goes into. They just come over
him all of a sudden and he doesn't have the slightest idea what he's doing. He's been to doctors about
it and everything. He had to write out a long case
history. You know. Gee, wouldn't it be awful to
have something like that the matter with you?"

"He ought to be put away," William said.

"But, gee, I think we ought to make an effort to
understand people like that and sympathize with
them, don't you?"

"No."

"He's really terribly sorry about what happened."

"Hand me that paper, will you?" said William.

"You're not mad at me anymore, are you?"

"No," said William. "Not at all."

They had a good fire burning before long. William cut some green branches on which to roast the
wieners. Dorothy was kneeling before the fire,

unwrapping packages, when he came back from the creek with the wine bottle. She had taken off her shoes.

"I guess it didn't have time to get very cold," he said. "You'll drink some wine, won't you?"

"I guess so. Just a little."

"We'll both have to drink out of the bottle."

"That's all right."

They had some wine and began to eat. It was very dark now and they put more wood on the fire before they ate the apples.

"Gee, I get so perplexed at times," Dorothy said.

"About what?"

"Oh, Life. I mean, most of the time I think Life is pretty wonderful, and then other times, all the trouble seems to pile up at once. Ingrid says that I wouldn't worry so much about things if I was a Communist. Do you think that's true?"

"Perhaps."

"She's only been a Communist for a little while. I think I can notice a difference."

"Can you?"

"Gee, when I was in Hollywood one time I got down to almost nothing at all. All I had was one dress and shoes and stockings and a hat and a toothbrush. I couldn't get any work and they kicked me out of my room. Well, I met a girl I knew at Central Casting and she invited me to a party. I was just starved and I'll bet I ate a hundred of those little tiny sandwiches. Did they ever taste good! I got to talking to a man there and he asked me to come live with him. Can you imagine! He had a marvelous apartment in Beverly Hills; he was a dress extra who always had work. But I couldn't understand why he wanted me to live with him because this girlfriend of mine told me he was a fairy.

"It was the craziest thing! He wasn't interested in me that way at all. I lived with him for three months and he never so much as laid a finger on me. The only thing was, he was always trying to get me to say a certain sentence, just a few words."

"What were they?"

"Gee, I couldn't bring myself to tell anybody that! It was awful! He'd get me in a corner and say, 'Now you've got to say it!' I never did, though. But he was simply perfect in every other way, and all I had to do was to keep the place clean and cook his breakfasts. He used to go down to San Luis Obispo a lot; I never did know what for. Or course, I had to leave when he brought certain of his friends in."

"Of course."

She looked at her apple core and then threw it into the fire. "I mean, gee, aren't some people strange, though!"

She lay back on the blanket and looked up at the sky. William drank some more wine and stretched out beside her. He lit cigarettes and gave her one.

They smoked for a while without speaking.

He kissed her on the throat and then on the mouth. She put her arms around him, throwing her cigarette away. They were very quiet for a while. The fire was burning out.

"I'm crazy about you," he said.

"Are you, Bill?"

"Yes. I'm crazy about you."

"You're sweet."

"Darling."

"Wait a minute."

"There, that's better."

"I shouldn't have been so nasty to you the other night."

"Don't think about it anymore."

"Bill?"

"Yes, darling."

"Do that some more."

"Like that?"

"Yes. Oh, darling."

The only light was the dying glow of the camp fire. Somewhere in the woods he could hear a bird singing. Then suddenly she pushed him away and sat up. "Oh God, what time is it?"

William was breathing heavily. "I don't know. What difference does it make?"

"Don't you have a watch?" she said. She was combing her hair and frowning at him intently.

"It must be about eight-thirty."

"Oh my God!"

They put out the fire and drove back to her place at a great rate. She did not volunteer any explanation. There was a man waiting for her in a car in front of the house. He got out when they drove up and walked over to them.

"Who is it? Baxter?" William whispered.

"Don't talk so loud. It's a boy I've got a date with. Gee, he looks perfectly furious."

Dorothy got out of the car at once and she and the man began to argue extendedly over how long he had been kept waiting. The man was very tall and spoke in guttural tones. In the darkness it was not possible to get a good idea of what he looked like.

William said good-bye through clenched teeth and left them on the curb. This was the end. A person could stand only so much. There were limits to what he would take. He would build a new life for himself and forget about her. No one, no one, could play fast-and-loose with William Clay indefinitely. He would go to Dr. Showers and demand that the burden of teaching the 101g's be distributed about more evenly. He was damned if he would be exploited any longer. He would construct an existence built upon love of work and ruthless self-interest.

At a drugstore he pulled up at the curb and went inside to buy another bottle of wine. As for Dorothy, there were plenty of fish in the sea. She didn't need to think she could walk all over him and expect him to applaud.

Back in his room, he sat wondering what would have happened had she not remembered her engagement. His anger had drained way. After all, he reflected, she *was* pretty wonderful. It had been marvelous there in the woods. A few minutes more and there would have been only the slightest possibility of interruption.

He uncorked the bottle and drank deeply. From now on, he resolved always to keep a bottle in his room. He wondered about her. Perhaps he was acting hastily when, after all, the situation was filled with promise in so many ways. Going over to the mirror, he stared at his reflections for a long time. He found it difficult to begin correcting the themes on "My Home Town."

FOURTEEN

It had been raining for hours. In the darkness of the afternoon the campus seemed to take on a sinister and foreboding atmosphere. A few bedraggled students hurried over the wet sidewalks, their books concealed beneath their raincoats. Lights were burning in the building. Water overflowed the gutters, carrying wet leaves.

William came away from the window and sat at his desk. The dampness seemed to penetrate the office. He wondered where Dorothy was and what she was doing and when he would see her again. He pursued this line of thought for some time and then he got up and emptied the ashtray, lit a cigarette and put his feet up on his desk. Once he reached for the telephone and then thought better of it.

He was quite incapable of coping with anything more this afternoon. A girl in one of his classes had attempted to become intimate during a conference. She wore a hair ribbon and had a dirty neck. It had been a delicate situation to handle, and he was not yet sure that he had done the right thing by pretending to be utterly dense. Fortunately the telephone had rung just when she had shown signs of becoming definitely aggressive.

None of the conferences, as a matter of fact, had been too successful. The Murdock boy still could not distinguish between a verb and a noun. William had tried everything with him. At any rate, William felt, Murdock actually wanted to be able to tell the difference, and that was more than he could say for most of them. It was impossible to get them to talk. When he had attempted to draw them out and discover their individual interests, in order to get them to choose their own theme subjects, they had become quite mute.

"Maybe they have no interests," he said aloud, putting out his cigarette and lighting another.

"Beg pardon?" said Mr. Waverly.

"Nothing," said William. "I was thinking out loud." He had forgotten Mr. Waverly entirely. It was easy to do that. Mr. Waverly had come in an hour ago, shortly after William's predicament with the girl, to settle down in his chair and gaze in a black mood at the rain, starting violently at each clap of thunder. Mr. Waverly had shared William's office for a week now. One of the buildings, Osgood Hall, condemned for years, was being razed. A student had stepped through a rotten board in one of the classrooms, broken his leg, and was suing the University. This had definitely decided those in authority that Osgood Hall must go. Their decision had necessitated a certain amount of doubling up among the faculty, and Mr. Waverly had moved in with William.

He was a very silent middle-aged man, exuding an odor of moth balls, with thick lenses in his glasses. An associate professor of Education, he had written numerous papers on the bladder control of the preschool child. Now and then he would look up as though about to deliver some arresting pronouncement, but nothing whatever came of these alarms. William had attempted conversation with him a number of times and, after very unsatisfactory results, ignored him as much as possible. He would have liked to have heard Mr. Waverly on his field of specialization, but did not know quite how to introduce the subject gracefully.

"Some rain," William said.

"Um," said Mr. Waverly, looking at it.

Irritably, William knocked ashes from his cigarette and put his feet down. Why had *he* been the one to draw Mr. Waverly? Forty-three men in Osgood Hall and he had the luck to be fixed up with this person. No one knew when construction of Murfin Hall, which would replace Osgood, would begin. Mr. Waverly might be with him for years.

William went down the hall. He was leaning over the drinking fountain when he heard Miss McVetchen calling his name.

"Oh, Mr. Clay! Mr. Clay! Hoo-hoo!"

"Oh, hello," he said, choking a bit as he swallowed the wrong way.

She began to hit him on the back. "Feel better?" she asked.

"Yes, much better, thank you."

"I just never see you any more. You're not avoiding me, I hope!"

"No, I've just been working pretty hard lately."

"You poor boy, you just don't look at all well these days. Did you know that? Your face is so drawn and you've lost so much weight. Now, look here, you've just got to come over to my place and let me feed you a lot of good home cooking; put some fat on those bones of yours."

"Do I really look bad?"

"Oh, I saw you in the hall the other day and I thought: They're working him too hard! Yes, I'm worried about you! And look at your fingers! See how yellow they are! You must be smoking far too much!"

"You think I'm thin, do you?"

"Oh, yes, yes!" said Miss McVetchen, shaking her head. She laid a hand on his arm and said in a low, confidential voice, "I suppose you've heard about poor Mr. Devlin."

"No. What about him?"

"You haven't heard?"

"No."

"They're letting him out at the end of the Fall quarter."

"Honestly?"

"So many complaints, I guess." Miss McVetchen looked over her shoulder. "Isn't it a shame, though? Such a brilliant mind and all the talent in the world. And he's such a marvelous teacher! But somehow it got to Dr. Showers that he hadn't met a single one of his eight o'clocks for two whole weeks! He'd told his students just not to come at all, he wouldn't be there. I heard he'd assigned a long paper and told them they would be expected to spend that hour in meditation."

"Poor Devlin."

"Now you must *do* something about yourself! And you must come over—soon!" William had begun to move in the direction of Devlin's office. "Saturday night! I'm having quite a crowd!"

"All right."

"Don't forget!"

Devlin was sitting in his office eating potato chips. From time to time he wiped at the back of his neck with a handkerchief. A pail in one corner of the room caught drops of water that fell with a metallic sound from a pipe overhead. A bitter-looking, but rather pretty dark girl sat by the window.

"Come on in," Devlin said as William hesitated. "This is my former wife. She just blew in. This is Mr. Clay, one of our embryo Bliss Perrys."

"How do you do," William said.

The girl frowned at him with indifference and turned to Devlin. "What do you think I am, anyway? If you think I'm going to leave quietly, Christopher Devlin, you can just think again. I'm going to stay right here until I get what I came for." She spoke as though repeating something she had said a hundred times before.

"You can't get blood out of a turnip," Devlin said. He looked at William. "Back alimony," he explained. "Just push those papers on the floor and sit down, William. Marjorie and I will be glad to have a referee, won't we, dear?"

"He owes me three hundred dollars," she said,

addressing William. "Can you imagine? Three hundred dollars, the worthless bum!"

"Please," said Devlin in a wounded manner. "Let's keep personalities out of this. As I said before, I don't have anything like that." He went to the door and closed it and came back to take a bottle of whiskey from a desk drawer. "Have a bit of the body builder, William?"

"No, thank you."

"No? . . . Marjorie?"

"No!"

Devlin had some. "I have eight dollars and fifty-nine cents, and you catch me in an affluent moment, at that. Nice of you to drop in just now, Marjorie, very nice indeed. You heard that our department head is tying the can to me, didn't you, Bill?"

"Miss McVetchen told me."

"How the news gets around. This had had the expert supervision of M. Cathcart Lund, I feel sure. Perhaps you'll have the pleasure of putting me in jail, my dear. You'd like that, wouldn't you?"

"You know damn well I would."

"Spoken like a little lady!" Devlin finished the potato chips and threw the sack in the wastebasket. To William he said, "You knew that Lund has reconsidered and isn't taking that job, didn't you? They raised his rank and his pay; can't let a valuable man like that escape. So he'll be with us, after all. With *you*, I should say."

Devlin's ex-wife said, "Christopher, just what do you do with your money, anyway?"

"What do I do with it?" Devlin looked up at the ceiling as though expecting to find the answer written there. "Why, I put it into the Devlin Foundation. I thought everyone knew that."

"You're not funny."

"You don't think so?"

William said, "I really must be going. I just stopped in to borrow some of those green slips."

"Form 154B?"

"Those are the ones."

"Fresh out."

"Never mind. It isn't important."

"Don't rush off. Marjorie is infinitely more sociable with someone else around. Aren't you, dear?"

Someone knocked at the door. It was Mr. Waverly.

"Clay in here?" Mr. Waverly's sight was imperfect. "Oh, hello," he said. "Someone named Showers called and wants you to come to his office right way. Think that was the name." Mr. Waverly turned and went down the hall. It was the longest utterance William had ever heard from Mr. Waverly.

"My God, what do you suppose he wants?" he said.

"Perhaps the axe will fall again."

"Do you think so?"

"I hope not, but one never knows."

"Well, I'd better get it over with."

"The best of luck."

"Very glad to have met you, Mrs. Devlin," William said.

"Good-bye," said Mrs. Devlin, taking off her shoe and shaking something from it.

Her voice began to rise as he closed the door. He stood for a time in the hall, feeling more than a little numb. This summons was very unnerving. Fantastic, too, that Devlin had never mentioned his marriage.

Dr. Showers was engaged in talking to a seedy-looking candidate for the Master's degree when William entered. He looked up and greeted William in a noncommittal manner. William sat down and looked past the Winged Victory at the rain outside. It appeared that the Master's candidate was doing a thesis on some etymological matter. The candidate kept glancing uncertainly at William. He had a speech impediment and had trouble keeping up his end of the conversation.

When he had gone, Dr. Showers said, "I shall be with you in a moment, Mr. Clay."

His manner seemed forbidding. William regarded the bust of Swift, his heart pounding.

Dr. Showers wrote for some time on a slip of paper, which he finally tossed on his desk among hundreds of other such slips. Clearing his throat, he removed his glasses and cleaned them with deliberate slowness. Then he put them back on, squinted, and turned in his chair to face William.

"I scarcely know how to begin," he said. "Two matters concerning yourself have come to my attention. Do you have any idea to what I refer?"

"No, sir."

"I see." Dr. Showers tapped his fingers on his desk in his best executive manner and appeared to be waiting for some further comment on William's part.

William regarded Dr. Showers with what he hoped was an air of incredulity and innocence. "Something I've done?" he asked.

"To speak bluntly, Mr. Clay, I have learned that you drink heavily and attend wild parties. Moreover, that you have appeared publicly in a drunken state. Do you deny it? I have learned of this from a source I consider entirely reliable, and I should like to know what you have to say. Are these accusations true?"

William felt blood mount in his face. "Well, no, not exactly, Dr. Showers. I've certainly done nothing I'm ashamed of. I suppose, on one occasion, I—was a bit . . ."

Dr. Showers was looking at him steadily. "I see. May I have your word that there shall be no repetitions?"

William nodded, looking at the floor.

"Very well, then. I shall not mention the matter

again. I try to be tolerant and I believe that I am;
but you realize, Mr. Clay, that tolerance must end
somewhere. Any repetitions and you understand
the position in which I shall be placed."

"Of course."

"I have been very disappointed in you, Mr. Clay,
extremely disappointed. You came here with the
highest recommendations, the very highest, and I
certainly expected nothing of this sort. To tell the
truth, I was shocked. Shocked."

"I can't tell you how sorry I am about this."

"The details that came to me were *most* unsavory."
Dr. Showers cleared his throat. "Very well, then.
We will consider the matter as closed. Now, about
this other." He frowned. "Let me see, what was it
now? Oh, yes. You have a student named Kunkle,
have you not?" He rummaged among his papers
and, like a magician triumphantly producing the chosen
card, brought forth a scrap of paper with a name
written on it. "Harold Kunkle," he said.

"Yes, I have a student by that name."

"You have turned him in as failing for the six weeks',
I understand."

"Why, yes, I have."

"And why did you do that?"

"Well, in the first place, he has handed in no papers."

"And in the second place?"

"He is without doubt among my five most stupid
students."

Dr. Showers moistened his lips and contemplated
the storm. He drummed his fingers on his knee.
"That grade must be changed," he said.

"Why, Dr. Showers?"

"You should have ascertained that he is the only
son of F. R. Kunkle, one of this institution's trustees." Dr. Showers stood up, crumpled the scrap of
paper and tossed it into the wastebasket with an air
of finality. "It is up to you, Mr. Clay, to see that
those papers come in and that Harold Kunkle re-
ceives a passing grade . . . Please leave the door
slightly ajar on your way out."

Devlin's wife had gone. Devlin was standing at
the window, scratching his leg and puffing at a cigar.
He turned as though with effort and said, "How
did you make out?"

William sat down. He had never felt in poorer
spirits. "What's your honest opinion of me?"

"I guess you didn't make out so good," Devlin
said, examining his cigar with faint distaste. "I thought
for a while maybe it was up the ladder of Fame for
you, too."

"Like Lund," William said.

"Like Lund."

"Nothing of the sort."

"Expand on the subject."

"He is very disappointed in me."

"Dr. Showers?"

"Dr. Showers."

"La!"

"I drink and attend wild parties; worst of all, I flunked Harold Kunkle for the six weeks'."

"Kunkle? Who's Kunkle? A nephew of Showers'?"

"The son of one of the trustees."

Devlin gave a low whistle. "I guess you slipped up that time. What's your next move?"

"I wish I knew."

Wind drove the rain in gusts across the campus. They watched Dr. Showers leave the building and hurry out to his car, his briefcase flopping against his leg.

"A splendid man," Devlin observed.

William said, "May I ask you something?"

"I wish you would."

"Do you know of any small, secluded bars?"

"Where you will not be observed?"

"That's what I mean."

"I know the very place," Devlin said, picking up his hat. "You voiced, as a matter of fact, my own unspoken thought."

Inside it was warm and dry and the radio was playing. From behind a thin wall came the sounds of billiard balls clicking against each other. William stared at a lithograph of a brewery that hung below a mangy elk's head. To one side of the elk dangled a red tissue-paper bell, dusty and water-spotted, memento of some distant and buried Christmas. A yeasty odor dominated the atmosphere.

"I could cite you many a coincidence," a man at the bar was saying. "Like the time Bubbles come in and knocked me halfway across the room. He was wearing his ruby ring."

"That Bubbles," a man with him said.

Devlin said, "What are we going to do about Lund?"

"Lund?"

"Yes, Lund. Let me have some more ice, Fred."

"Well, what *can* we do about him?"

"During the Middle Ages the boys knew a trick or two."

Fred, an obese man in a soiled apron, moved heavily over to their booth and put more ice in Devlin's glass.

"Good of you, Fred."

"Not at all."

"Good of you, though."

"I could cite you many a coincidence," the man at the bar said. "You don't know nothing about the cops in this town."

"To hell with Lund," William said.

"What a way to talk," said Devlin.

"To hell with Showers. I wish someone would tell me why we had to get into this profession in the first place."

"Now you're talking sense."

William emptied his glass.

"Of course we wouldn't be in it, if we were capable of doing anything else," Devlin said.

"I'll have another of these."

"Two more."

The men at the bar went out. William listened to the radio. "Isn't that Dorothy singing?" he said.

"So it is."

They sat in silence until she had finished and an announcer had given a glowing account of a mouthwash.

"She's marvelous," William said.

"As a vocalist, you mean?"

William stared into space. "What was it we were talking about?"

"I don't recall. It couldn't have been of much significance." Devlin made rings on the table with his glass. "Well, here's to John Dewey," he said.

"To John Dewey," William said. "Are you sure this is a very secluded bar?"

"They don't come any more secluded than the Lilac Grill. This place is known only to a few cognoscenti."

"I hope you're right."

"Would I lie to you?" Devlin said. "It seems to me you're awfully suspicious these days. To Alvin E. Pope."

"Do I know him?"

"Superintendent of the New Jersey School for the Deaf."

They drank for a while. There were noises from the adjoining room suggesting that someone was hitting someone else over the head with a pool cue.

"I guess she isn't going to sing anymore," William said.

"Two more," Devlin said. "What's the matter, has she been giving you the runaround?"

"I was sort of engaged to a girl once," said William. "Name of Frances."

"I knew a girl named Frances. Frances Fitzwater. Pretty name. Nothing ever came of that."

"There were some people named Fitzwater at home. All the boys were in reform school."

"That reminds me. I'll have to get off a letter to the Mizpah Agency before long."

"Are they good?"

"No."

"Why do you patronize them?"

"They ask no questions."

"I see."

"I guess I'll have to let Marjorie have my stock in the diamond mine. She'd love to get her hands on that. All I have left of my inheritance. But you don't want to hear about my domestic difficulties," Devlin said, raising his glass. "To Elwood P. Cubberly."

"To Elwood P. Cubberly," William said.

"One nice detail,"Devlin said. "The University has to give me two months' pay for breaking my contract."

"That's something."

"It's the least they could do."

"I should think so."

"I really feel quite good about it, suddenly," Devlin said.

William had been listening to the radio. "No," he said. "I guess she isn't going to sing anymore. Let's drink to somebody."

"Let me think," said Devlin, scrutinizing the threadbare cuff of his shirt.

FIFTEEN

He let Devlin out of the car in front of his apartment house. Devlin stood on the sidewalk, his face wet, looking up at a window. He had been silent for a good many blocks.

"The little woman will be up there, no doubt," he said.

"What about the three hundred dollars?"

Devlin pursed his lips. "I feel a plan coming on."

"The stock in the diamond mine?"

"That enters into it."

"See you tomorrow."

"You may, at that."

He closed the door and went up the steps a trifle unsteadily. William drove down the street, intending to go home; then, acting upon a sudden impulse, he turned towards town. In front of the Hotel Hubbard he parked and glanced at a clock in a drugstore window. He turned off the motor and lit a cigarette.

In the Lilac Grill, as Devlin had insisted the bar was named, William had felt momentarily on the verge of intoxication, but now his head was clear and, as he held out his hand to study it, it shook hardly at all. Steady as can be, he thought. He pulled the mirror down and looked at his tongue. It could have been far worse.

He did not have long to wait. It was scarcely five minutes before she came out through the revolving door and stood uncertainly under the awning, looking up the street. She was wearing a beret and a trench coat.

William got out of the car and went over to her.

"Hello," he said.

"Oh hello, Bill," she said rather tonelessly. "What are you doing here?"

"Get in the car."

"Where are we going?"

"Up to your place."

"Are you drunk?"

"Not in the least."

She did not speak for a while and William watched the windshield wiper clicking back and forth and the rain slanting past the headlights.

She said, "I'm never going back there again."

"Where?"

"To the station. I'll never go back there if I can help it."

"What happened?"

"Oh, I'm so fed up with everything. Fed up! They've got this new program director, a woman. Red-haired and bony and oh God you can't imagine how mean she is."

"So?"

"So they can just struggle along without me." Suddenly her manner changed. Moving over close to him, she dropped her head on his shoulder and began to cry. "I can't help it! Nobody can talk to me like that! Nobody! I've got feelings! She can't treat me that way!"

"There, there," William said.

"Oh, it's been such a devil of a day!"

"I guess everybody's been getting it."

"Oh, Bill, be sweet to me."

"Darling. Here, have a handkerchief."

"I've got one. Why does everything have to happen to me? I was getting along all right, perfectly all right. And then she had to come along."

"It'll be all right."

For a moment he thought how fine it would be if they could just keep on driving forever, on and on and on, away from the University and Dr. Showers and Harold Kunkle and all the rest of it, and there would be the endless road and many places they could go, and she would be in love with him and never look at anyone else. It was soothing to dwell upon, but he remembered to make the right turn for her apartment house.

There were two bills for her in the mailbox. She opened them at the bottom of the stairs as though they constituted some immense and final affront. Stuffed them in the pocket of her coat with a weary gesture and they went up the stairs.

"A man was strangled here last week, Bill," she said. "Did you hear about it?"

"I read about it in the paper."

"It happened while I was gone."

"With a stocking, wasn't it?"

"I think so."

She had stopped crying and fumbled in her purse for the key and unlocked the door. Gray light came in at the window. As though unaware of him, she dropped to the bed and kicked off her shoes. He took off his coat and hat and came over to her.

"Don't feel badly about it," he said. He felt tender and responsible. Caressing her, he found her to be completely passive. She looked up at him with large eyes.

"Oh, Bill, I'm so glad you're here. Sometimes I can't stand being alone."

"You're sweet."

"Lock the door."

"It's locked."

"Sure?"

"Positive."

"Help me with this."

He could not escape the feeling that it should have involved more difficulty. In the early evening, the rain still continued to fall, a steady and incessant downpour; and in the room, where no lights burned, a wet and somehow not unpleasant darkness had settled over everything. A radio somewhere in the house moaned briefly as though in pain. He raised one arm and felt for the light switch by the bed and turned it on.

Her quarters, one room and a bath, gave the impression of impermanence, as though she had just moved in and did not plan to remain for long. There were just a few books stacked on the dresser, mostly treatises on the cultivation of the human voice, one on writing for radio, one on color and several best-sellers of a few years back. On the wall was a recently-executed oil painting of two nude women. They were examining a cluster of grapes with an air of wonder. The women bore a faint resemblance to

Dorothy and Ingrid Spitalnick. Something glinted by the window and he realized that he was looking at a bowl of goldfish.

From the distance came the sound of a train whistle, faint through the rain, and William was stirred with a sense of languor and exhaustion and peace. Now, however, he was beginning to feel a trifle chilly. A draught came in through the transom. He pulled a blanket over them, looking down at Dorothy. One of her arms lay over his chest and her eyes were closed.

He listened to the rain beating on the roof.

"Are you asleep?" he asked.

"No."

"All right now?"

"Yes." She opened her eyes.

"Did you mean what you said about the station?"

"About not going back?"

"Yes."

"I meant it, all right."

"What are you going to do?"

"I don't know. I'm not going to worry about it. Something will come up. That's the cutest mole. What a funny place to have one."

"Dorothy," he said, very tenderly.

"Yes."

"Why don't you marry me?"

She looked up at him, startled, and when she did not reply, he said, "If we were married, I wouldn't care what my work was like. It wouldn't matter anymore."

"Oh, Bill, why did you have to ask me? We were getting along so nicely."

"What do you mean?"

"I just can't do it."

He felt that something was coming out that he did not want to hear. "Why not?"

"I just can't."

"But why can't you?"

"I'm not in any position to. You see, well, I'm not divorced."

"That actor, you mean? I thought you told me you were divorced from him."

"Carl? Oh, not Carl. I mean the second boy I married."

"The second one?"

"Yes. Didn't you know I was married twice?"

"I had no idea."

"It was sweet of you to ask me but, I don't know, after you've been married a couple of times and it didn't work out either time, you get to wondering whether it's worth it or not."

"I suppose."

"You become so skeptical."

"What was he like?"

"Who?"

"Your second husband."

"He was a salesman. He sold Red Heart Dog Food."

"How long ago was this?"

"Two years ago. We should never have got married in the first place. He didn't understand me at all and I guess I wasn't steady enough for him or something. That's what he said, anyway. He used to say all the time that I was 'failing him.' Do you want me to tell you something? He was tattooed on his back. A big American flag." She leaned on her elbow and her hair fell over to one side. "Oh gosh, sometimes I get so sick of it all. I want to make a clean start, Bill. A clean start. Wipe the slate clean and start all over again."

"So would I."

"Would you really? Gosh, though, you seem so adjusted, I don't know, so well-balanced!"

"Do you think I am?"

"That's the sweetest mole."

He told her about his interview with Dr. Showers. "The whole business is exasperating," he said. "It's bad enough to have to put up with the 101g's, but this Kunkle thing is too much to swallow."

"I don't see how that Showers has the nerve! Why, he must be a terrible person!" She became momentarily infected by his own disgust and then lay back and contemplated the ceiling. A thoughtful look came over her face. "Bill, can you keep a secret?"

"What is it?"

"Well, nobody must know. Nobody."

"You have my word."

"Promise?"

"Promise."

"Well, I told you I didn't have anything in mind about what I was going to do. But there is something. You see, Annabelle Shanahan's sister died— ptomaine, she had even more money than Annabelle, *very* wealthy—and she left her everything. Well, in a way, that upset Annabelle's plans, because she's been planing to go to Buenos Aires for the winter and now she's got all kinds of things to settle up. And there's the little boy, too."

"What little boy?"

"Her little nephew, her sister's child. Annabelle wants to get a governess for him, and I think I've just about talked her into the idea of giving me the job. Gosh, wouldn't that be perfectly wonderful! Living in Buenos Aires!"

"You'd be going away," William said.

"But listen!" Dorothy said. "I'm not through yet. Annabelle wants to get a tutor for little Raymond, too."

"The boy."

"Yes."

"I see what you're getting at."

"Gosh, wouldn't it be marvelous if we could work it!"

"How old is he?"

Dorothy was rather vague about this. "Oh, I don't know—seven or eight, I guess."

"He couldn't possibly be worse than the 101g's."

"Why didn't I think of it before? Gee, I think you'd be just what she'd want! She likes you, I know. Isn't it the swellest idea! Buenos Aires! And Annabelle wouldn't care whether we were married or not."

They lay in bed making plans. William had not experienced elation of this sort for some time. Nevertheless, he reasoned that it would be well to consider the idea from every angle. He did not speak of this to Dorothy, however. William was all too well-trained in academic caution to take to the plan wholeheartedly. That he had got off to a bad start at the University was undeniable, but he still clung, rather pathetically, to a belief that the career of a college teacher was not without its rewards.

It had been his misfortune to take a job at the wrong school, that was all. Conditions there, he felt sure, were simply not representative. He might do far worse than to go to Buenos Aires, in the meanwhile writing carefully-worded letters to schools and agencies and lining up a position worthy of his talents.

After a while she got up and went to the bathroom. William dressed in haste so that she would not come back while he was engaged in fastening his clothing. In a room in a house next door, two people appeared to be measuring each other with a yardstick. One of them was a man with a beard.

The other wore a fez and dark glasses. He watched them for a while and then pulled the shade and sat looking at diagrams of the larynx in one of Dorothy's books.

Before long she came out, dressed in a sweater and slacks.

"You can go in now," she said.

When he emerged, she was breaking up fish food and dropping it in the water. "Gosh, they must be starved. I just about forgot to feed them. Look at them go for it! I'm kind of hungry myself."

William said, "Whose painting is that?"

"Mine. Do you like it? It's the first oil I ever did. That's me, and this is Ingrid."

"I thought I noted a resemblance."

"I'm going to do a nude of her alone next. She has a *lovely* body. Gosh, you don't know the thrill of painting, Bill! Really! It's marvelous, simply marvelous. There must be wonderful things to paint down in Buenos Aires, wouldn't you imagine? They say it's just terribly colorful down there."

"It must be fine," he said. "Do you want to go downtown and eat?"

She was making sure the fish were well provided for. "Oh, why do that? We can go in and see if Ingrid hasn't got something for us."

There were few things he wanted to do less than to see Ingrid Spitalnick.

"Oh, let's not."

"It won't be any imposition."

"Let me take you to dinner."

"Why, Bill, don't you like Ingrid?"

"I can't say that I do."

"Gee, you've got to get over that! Why, Ingrid is a terribly interesting person."

"Please. Let's eat downtown."

"Don't be impossible, Bill. Are you coming or aren't you?"

He followed her, irritated with her and angry with himself for not making more of an issue of it. He was surprised, in view of Dorothy's ultimatum that no one should know of their plans, that almost the first words she spoke to Ingrid Spitalnick were connected with them. Ingrid had been pretending to read a thick book of a Left-wing nature when they came in, and she said that the political scene in Bolivia was very complex though encouraging. She had, come to think of it, read something only the other day about the situation there. It was all a matter of time, anyway. It would certainly be fascinating, she said, to observe it at first hand.

William attempted to point out that Buenos Aires was not in Bolivia, but Argentina; Dorothy and Ingrid, however, had begun to converse in the feverishly intense manner of intimates who have much to talk over. From the kitchen, Ingrid Spitalnick kept casting glances of a meaningful nature his way. He sat down, more and more annoyed, tapping his foot and taking deep breaths.

The food, when it arrived, was scarcely edible. They ate at a card table, one leg of which threatened to push in at any moment.

"Oh, Dorothy, the new District Organizer came today," Ingrid said. "He's the sweetest man! He showed us the loveliest pictures of some Soviet bombers!"

"Ingrid, you mustn't get in too deep with those people," Dorothy said.

"I've made up my mind. I'm definitely going to join the Party."

"Ingrid, are you really?"

"Of course I will always believe that there is a place for Beauty and nothing will interfere with our painting lessons."

"Gee, I should hope not!"

"The D.O. has had fascinating experiences. He promised to show me the scars he got in a riot in Chicago."

"You should be careful, though, Ingrid."

"Don't you like the haddock á la créme, Mr. Clay? Here, eat what you have and let me give you some more."

"No, thank you."

"Oh, Dorothy, I hate to think of you going off to Buenos Aires! I'll be so lonesome around here."

"You'll have the Party, though."

"Oh, yes, there will be that, of course," Ingrid said.

"I do wish you could meet Comrade Olson. I don't know *when* I've been in the presence of such a dynamic personality."

"What's he like?"

"Very blonde and enthusiastic. He has great plans for the agricultural proletariat." They finished their coffee and she stacked the dishes and took off the apron she had been wearing. "Have you seen that cross-eyed boy lately?"

"Not for a few days."

"It's a shame his eyes are crossed. So good-looking, otherwise. Have you met him, Mr. Clay?"

"No."

"Only one of his eyes is crossed, really. You scarcely notice it except close up. *Very* handsome."

Dorothy did not seem to care for the direction the conversation was taking. "Well, let's go if we're going," she said. "I'll get my coat."

"Is it time?"

William said, "Where is it we're going?"

"To Chester Thompson's. Didn't you know? This is the night for our lesson. You can drive us over."

"That road will be bad."

"Do you think so?" Dorothy said.

They went out to the car. It had stopped raining and the night air was cold. Ingrid Spitalnick elected to sit in the front seat between William and Dorothy. Her legs were even longer than he had dared to imagine and made shifting the gears something of a feat.

Dorothy talked most of the way about the red-haired program director, accompanied by commiserations from Ingrid, who suggested that the time was not far off when such people would be deprived of their power.

"Oh, Ingrid, I just can't help feeling that human nature does not change," Dorothy said.

Ingrid Spitalnick attempted to correct her for taking such views and William stopped to buy cigarettes. Intense shooting pains in his stomach had begun and he had a Bromo Seltzer in the drugstore. He should never have touched the haddock in the first place. When he came back they were discussing a henna bath Dorothy had once taken. It had not turned out as she had hoped and had left her body peculiarly mottled.

"Gee, it seemed like such a good idea, too!" Dorothy said. "I think I must have done something wrong."

"Here's the turn," Ingrid Spitalnick said.

"Why, the road doesn't look bad at all!" said Dorothy.

It was almost impassable. On several occasions, William felt sure they were stuck for the night. Mud covered the entire car. Once they almost went in the ditch. He was perspiring and exhausted when the car finally stopped at One Dewey Drive.

"I'll get out first," he said. "It looks as though it might be less muddy here than on your side."

He stepped with caution and it seemed firm enough, but when he put his whole weight down, he sank in mud to his knees. He was wearing his newest suit. The girls began to laugh but stopped almost at once and began to apologize. It was too late. William was furious. Getting back in the car, he slammed the door and drove up in front of the doorway. Chester Thompson came down the stairs as he turned off the motor.

"Hello, Chester!" said Dorothy and Ingrid.

Chester Thompson was in a happy mood. He had some yellow paint on his forehead, which gave him a festive appearance. He slapped William on the back. "Well, I certainly didn't think you'd make it tonight, girls, the way the roads are and all. Got a chauffeur, eh? Come on up and take a look at my new picture. Best damned thing I ever did! Got a flavor about it like Bosch, know what I mean?"

"What is it, Chester?"

"Row on row of coffins, see? Real architectural interest. And a bleak gray sky with vultures hovering overhead. Wait'll you see it! And then—listen—when you get close, you can make out the features of the people in the coffins." He paused for dramatic effect. "Every one of them is some guy I don't like." He smiled. "What do you think of that? Not bad, eh?"

"Chester, it's simply macabre!" said Ingrid Spitalnick.

"Come on up and see it! How about you? What is your name, anyway? I've got a terrible memory for names."

William looked at him. "Here's your handbag," he said to Dorothy.

"Aren't you coming up?" she asked.

"No."

"Jesus, you got kind of muddy, didn't you?" Chester Thompson said, looking at William's trousers.

"Yes," William said. "I got kind of muddy."

"It's marvelous the way Dorothy always manages to get somebody to drive her out here," Chester Thompson said. "Well, what are we standing around here for?" He grabbed Dorothy around the waist and pulled her over to him. "Say, you're pretty cute, aren't you?"

The three were talking busily about egg tempera as they went up the stairs. William remembered that nothing had been settled about the tutoring position, and he wondered if Dorothy wished him to apply directly to Annabelle Shanahan. "Dorothy!" he called up the stairs.

She was much too busy listening to Chester Thompson to hear him. He called again, louder, but by that time they had reached the top of the stairs and had gone inside and closed the door.

SIXTEEN

It was not until a week later that he saw her again.

For six days she dropped out of sight. William called
her on Friday and was told that she did not answer.
He received similar reports each time he called,
although his informants varied. Sunday night, not
finding her in, he drove in aimless melancholy through
the town, stopping every half hour to knock at her
door. Near midnight, he parked across the street
and waited, smoking one cigarette after another. He
fell asleep around two o'clock and was awakened
by a policeman, intent upon arresting him for drunk-
enness. The policeman was cajoled into smelling
his breath and let him off with some reluctance. It
had been a quiet night for the policeman. William
parked on another street and returned once more,
but there was no response to his rapping.

Although he left messages for her to call him, no
word came. Ingrid Spitalnick seemed equally difficult to find, but the night after his experience with
the policeman, noticing a light burning in her window as he drove by, he parked and climbed the stairs.
It was not late but he had to knock several times
before Ingrid opened the door an inch or two and
looked out.

"What do you want?"

"I'm looking for Dorothy."

"Well, you won't find her here."

"Do you know where she's gone?"

"I haven't the faintest idea."

"How long has it been since you've seen her?"

"I haven't seen her since the night after we went over to Chester's."

"She didn't leave any message, did she?"

"Not with me she didn't."

The door closed and he thought he heard whispering in the room. The man who was alleged to be a peddler of marijuana tipped his hat to William as he went down the hall. Two blowsy women in kimonos were talking under a light on the lower floor. "And then the butcher tried to cop a quick feel when he came around to show me the pot roast," one of them said. "We was all alone in the store."

"The one with the wen?" the other said delightedly.

"That's the baby."

No one at the radio station knew where Dorothy was, nor did Mrs. Diego Shanahan or Chester Thompson. It was, on the whole, a very bad week, marked also by an incipient temper tantrum on William's part during a class, a dull Saturday evening at Miss McVetchen's, at which word games were played, and by the blank refusal of Harold Kunkle to hand in his papers. William sent a note over to the office, requesting that Harold Kunkle's grade be changed to a D+.

In the gray mornings of the autumn between his first class and the one at ten o'clock it was gloomy but not unpleasant to sit at his desk and gaze out of the window at the slate-colored sky and the pass-

ing students, although the omission of some ingre-
dient in the plaster caused a shower of fine white
dust to fall from the ceiling now and then and made
him cough. Mr. Waverly was gone during this hour
and William was rarely interrupted from his soli-
tary thoughts.

At this time Thursday he called Dorothy's apartment house and was told by a none too affable woman
that she could be reached at another number, which
she gave him. He dialed the number and a man's
voice said, "Hotel Riggs." William inquired for Miss
Bruce but had to describe her before the call went
through. She answered in a sleepy voice.

"Hello."

"Hello! Dorothy? What's happened to you, anyway?"

"Who is this? Don? . . . Eric?"

"This is Bill—William Clay."

"Oh, hello."

"Where have you been?"

"What?"

"I say, where have you been?"

"Oh, out of town," she said. Her voice was cas-
ual. "Gee, what time is it? Do you have to call so
early in the morning?"

"Why didn't you let me know you were going?
I've been awfully worried about you."

"Didn't you get the note I sent you?"

"I didn't get any note."

"Didn't you? That's funny."

"Are you sure you sent it? Where did you go?"

"I'm positive I sent it." She did not answer the other question.

"Are you all right? Lord, I didn't know what had happened to you. By the way, had there been trouble between you and Ingrid Spitalnick? She was curt as the devil to me the other night."

"I don't know what's the matter with her. As far as I'm concerned, she's become simply impossible." She yawned audibly. "Bill, do you mind? You got me out of bed."

"When can I see you? Tonight?"

"Not tonight. Tomorrow night, maybe."

"Not until then?"

"Call before you come over. Something may come up."

"I'm sorry I got you out of bed—"

He heard the connection being broken. He put the receiver back and looked up at a man who had just entered. It was Mr. Bisbee of the Speech Department.

"Good morning!" Mr. Bisbee said brightly.

Mr. Bisbee's expression would have been interesting if he had had any. He had a smooth blank face over which no sign of feeling had ever been known to pass, although he expressed such emotions as he had through bodily movements of a disturbing order. He had very large ears which looked as though they had been carved from some gritty substance, and habitually wore blue serge suits that were too large for him, as though he expected in time to grow into them.

"Just dropped around to tell you we'd be awfully happy if you'd come around to try out for a part in the faculty play," he said.

"I see."

"You know about the faculty play, of course."

"No, I'm afraid I don't."

"It's an annual event." Mr. Bisbee pulled up a chair. "This year we're going to do Peer Gynt. Ibsen. Somewhat ambitious, you'll think, but there had been a good deal of criticism of the farces we've done in recent years—particularly the one last year in which Dr. Frognall ran across the stage without his trousers. We thought we'd go in for something heavier this time. Of course, it's what I've always recommended."

The first bell rang. "I have a class in a moment," William said, gathering some books and papers together.

"Naturally we are eager to enlist the forces of some of the new people on the campus, and of course we thought of you, Mr. Burton. For no particular role, you understand; but we should like you to come to the tryouts next Monday. Room 303, Amphlett Hall."

"My name is Clay. Burton was my predecessor."

Mr. Bisbee's arms fluttered around him. "Really?

You're not Burton?"

"No."

"You're quite serious?"

"He left last year. I'm afraid it would be out of the question, anyway, since I suffer from stage fright."

"I felt sure you were Burton. I had no idea he had left. If you have stage fright, though, all the more reason why you should come out and get over it. And it will be a sumptuous production."

"I'm sure that it will." Some of the dust from the ceiling was falling on Mr. Bisbee. It showed up well on his blue suit. "Will you excuse me now?" William said. "I'd better get to my class."

"You know those lines of Peer's at the end?" Something approaching an expression appeared in Mr. Bisbee's eyes. "'Mother and wife! You stainless woman! Oh, hide me, hide me in your love!' Remember?"

Mr. Waverly and one of his students, coming from a class, stood apprehensively in the doorway. William went down the hall to the classroom, leaving Mr. Bisbee to tell Mr. Waverly and his student about the play tryouts. Quite a lot of dust from the ceiling was falling on them by now.

He telephoned her the following evening and she said she would wait for him. He drove to the hotel. The branches of the trees were now bare and he could sense the approach of winter. The hotel was in the lower downtown district, not far from the railroad yards, a drab gray frame building.

An old woman with her false teeth out was sitting in the lobby crocheting what looked like a noose. A scrawny cat stretched itself on the window ledge near a potted fern. Near the open-cage elevator, a man with a cigar was reading the comic section of the newspaper. The desk clerk wore black sleeve protectors and looked up from a crossword puzzle.

"Miss Bruce?" William said.

"Who's that?"

"Miss Bruce, Dorothy Bruce."

He shook his head. "Nobody by that name staying here."

"She must be. Good-looking girl, about five feet two, around twenty-three or four."

"Oh, you must mean Mrs. Anderson. She's in 207."

William got in the elevator and the man reading the comics folded his paper with a tired air and followed him. The man closed the gate and pushed a lever and the cage crawled upward to the second floor.

"Watch your step," he said.

William walked down the hall. The carpets were worn. A red light burned near the fire escape and there was an axe in the box on the wall. A man in a bathrobe came out of a room carrying a towel and entered another room. It was difficult to see the

numbers on the doors and William found it necessary to walk up and down the hall several times
before he located the right one. He knocked and
she called for him to come in.

She was standing by the window staring outside
and turned as he came in. She was wearing a black
dress and looked pale and tired.

He put his arms around her and kissed her. She
seemed very small.

"Darling, what's the matter?" he said. "What's
happened? Where have you been?"

She had been crying. "Oh, Bill, I'm so sick of myself!
I'm so sick of everything!"

"Darling."

"I've got to get out of this town."

"We'll get out of it."

She began to cry again and he helped her over to
the bed and gave her a piece of Kleenex he found
on the dresser. After a while she stopped crying and
sat, red-eyed, twisting the Kleenex and biting her
lips.

"What in God's name are you doing in this rat
hole?" he said.

She giggled. "It is pretty terrible, isn't it?" As
though to regain control of herself, she blew her nose
violently. "There. I'm over that now. I promise
not to cry again. I don't know why I'm crying,
anyway."

Down the passageway someone was pounding on
the wall and he heard the elevator creaking on its

way up.

"Go ahead if it makes you feel any better," William said.

"No, I'm all over it now. Really. Will you take me for a ride? Just a little one, though; I can't go for very long."

She washed her face and put on fresh makeup and they went down to the car. A cold wind was blowing and some men were carrying garbage cans down the alley from the back door of a restaurant. He drove across the tracks and the bridge to the other side of town, the lights shining in the houses below them.

She lit a cigarette and he noticed how her hand shook. It was her last cigarette. She crushed the package and dropped it out of the window. After a time she said, "Do you still want to go to Buenos Aires?"

"Yes."

"Do you?"

"I think I do."

"I wonder if you do."

Ahead of them a car backfired. A badger's tail floated from a long metal rod attached to the back fender and there was a sticker pasted on the rear window that said, "Vote for Finlayson. Vote Progressive." The car climbed the slight elevation and turned off, its taillight blinking.

"Bill?"

"Yes."

"Do you love me?" she said.

"You know that."

"You don't really. You wouldn't if you knew about me."

"I know about you."

"Not really."

"Don't I?"

"You don't know anything. Do you want me to tell you?"

"No."

They passed the city limits sign and turned off on a graveled road. The headlights picked out a broken fence and a clump of osage orange bushes. A truck sounded its horn and went by them, raising a cloud of dust.

Dorothy said, "You know this new District Organizer that Ingrid was talking about? Erik Anderson?"

"I thought his name was Olson."

"He uses that, too," she said. "He uses half a dozen names. They have to." She took a deep breath. "Well, the night after you took us out to Chester's, he came over to see Ingrid about getting out some pamphlets or something. I won't go into all the details, but I guess he took quite a fancy to me and after a while Ingrid got sleepy and wanted to go to bed and so we went in my room." She cranked the window down carefully and threw her cigarette away. "Oh, golly, what a night, Bill! Gee, you can't imagine the way it was. My second husband—I guess I told you about him—well, he had to pick just that time to put in an appearance.

"Erik and I were just sitting there talking when all of a sudden somebody started pounding on the door and yelling for me to let him in. I didn't know it then, but he was terribly drunk and simply furious because he'd had so much trouble finding where I lived, and something else happened, I never did get that part of it straight. Well, we didn't know who it was, that time of night and everything, and we weren't going to let him in and he just about broke down the door and then he and Erik had the most horrible fight you can imagine. Blood all over everything, tore up my room; they were all up and down the hall. Everybody in the house was awake by then, and of course after it was all over I couldn't very well go back, although the manager was nice and said it wasn't my fault. They were fighting on the stairs when Erik knocked him out with his shoe. Can you imagine? He knocked Frank down the stairs and then got his shoe off and hit him a terrible whack with the leather heel. The blood was streaming down his head and they took him to a hospital. Erik brought me down to the hotel afterwards and I helped bandage him.

"Didn't I tell you I got involved?" she said. "Didn't I tell you?"

William turned the car around.

"Why did he register you as Mrs. Anderson?"

"Did he? I didn't know that. Where are we going?"

"I think we'd better go back and see Mrs. Shanahan."

"I can't go."

"Why not?"

"I just can't. What time is it?"

"A little after eight."

"Is it really? I've got to get right back to the hotel."

"Why won't you go with me? What do you have
to do?"

"Bill, I can't go, that's all. I've got a simply terrible headache. You can go over there if you want
to, but I wouldn't make any definite plans if I were
you."

"What do you mean?"

She avoided looking at him as he stopped in front
of the hotel. "Oh, you know how Annabelle is—so
terribly erratic. Gee, you just can't depend on anything she says."

"But you've been making plans. This Buenos Aires
thing was your idea."

"Oh, let's not talk about it any more now. I don't
know what to do." She rested her fingers on the
handle of the door and watched a man with a basket cross the street. "Could you loan me some money?"

"How much do you need?"

"Would twenty-five dollars be too much?"

He took out his wallet. "Twelve is all I have."

"That'll be all right."

"I can get some more for you in the morning."

"No, this is plenty."

"And see if you can't find some other place to live."

"Oh, don't worry about that. Good-bye, Bill. You're sweet. I must run now." She put the money in her purse. "I'll call you—in the morning, I guess."

"Kiss me."

She put her arms around his neck and kissed him lightly. He tried to hold her and kiss her again, but she opened the door and got out, smiling in a way he thought strange.

"Gee," she said, "it's sprinkling again."

"Is it?"

"Good-bye."

"Do you really have to go?"

"Yes, I've got to."

He watched her cross the street and enter the hotel and step into the elevator, after pausing to say something to the man at the desk. Then, worried and disturbed, he drove up the street in the light rain that had begun to fall.

SEVENTEEN

William went up to the porch and rang the doorbell, looking at the stone lions until Iams opened the door.

"Oh, good evening, Mr. Clay. Nice to see you again."

"Good evening, Iams. Is Mrs. Shanahan here?"

"I believe that she is engaged just at the moment, but won't you come in and wait?"

The living room was brightly lighted. Four people, strangers to William, were playing bridge there. The two women were apparently twins who had been exposed to diverse environments. One of them was burned a dark tan and spoke with a Southern accent, while the other, by comparison, seemed abnormally pale and could not be understood at all because of markedly British inflections. The men were smoking cigars and one of them wore medals on his coat.

"It has never occurred to any of them," the man with the medals said as he shuffled the cards, "that there is not going to be any war. War, war, that's all you hear in Europe. The more they rearm, the less likelihood there is of actual fighting. All bluff, I tell you."

The woman with the British accent looked at William through a lorgnette.

"Would you care to wait in the den?" Iams suggested.

"Yes, I think that would be better."

He followed Iams down the hall. Evidently Mrs. Shanahan was having an evening at the kettledrums, for the distant booming that he had heard before was plainly distinguishable.

"I'm sure she won't be long," Iams said. "May I get you a drink, Mr. Clay?"

"No, thank you, Iams."

"And how is Mr. Devlin these days?"

"Fairly well. He has been dismissed at the University, you know."

"Indeed? I hadn't known. I'm very sorry to hear that."

"It's a pity, certainly."

"It is that," Iams said, removing some infinitesimal object from the arm of a chair. "I always looked forward to his visits. Please don't hesitate to ring if you should change your mind about a drink, Mr. Clay."

William sat before the fire and looked at the painting of Dorothy. He still retained his admiration for it, but it was now tempered by the passage of time and by a fuller understanding of Chester Thompson. The noise from above grew in volume and William wondered if Mrs. Shanahan were using heavier drumsticks these days or merely exerting more pressure. It was clear, at any rate, that the soundproof room was not a success.

He leaned back and closed his eyes. It was pleasant to sit here by the fireside. He thought about Dorothy and wondered what she and Anderson had actually been doing when her second husband had beaten on the door. He tried to think about something else but recurring visual images kept forming in his mind.

Something that stung painfully hit him on the cheek. He clapped his hand to his face and looked about the room. A dreadful little boy was smiling fiendishly at him from behind a chair.

"Hit you, didn't I?" he said.

William dug his fingernails into the palms of his hands. This, without a doubt, was Raymond. "Yes, you hit me, all right," he managed to say.

"You jumped a foot," Raymond said. "These are sure keen rubber bands."

"And what do you use for ammunition?"

"Tinfoil. It's the best."

"I'm sure it is."

"You sure looked funny when I let you have it. I was aiming at your eye." The boy crawled out from where he had been hiding. He had a mass of weedy brown hair and a small, cruel mouth. One of his ears was larger than the other. He wore an Indian suit.

"What do you think of my outfit?" he asked.

"Very fine."

"I got it for being a good boy."

"I can't imagine how that happened."

"Oh, I was just good for a day and Annabelle bought it for me. Then that night I spit cod-liver oil all over Iams' pants."

"That wasn't a nice thing to do."

"Why wasn't it? It's awful stuff." He pulled the rubber band back and forth in an experimental manner. "Do you know those people in the front room?"

"No."

"That's Mr. and Mrs. Stokes and Major Fosdick-Browne and the woman he sleeps with."

"What a thing to say, Raymond."

"How did you know my name? She's Mrs. Stokes's sister. You ought to see their car! It's even keener than the one my mother had. Are you Mr. Prouty?"

"No, I'm Mr. Clay."

"Do you have a car?"

"Yes."

"A big one?"

"No, rather small."

"I thought maybe you were Mr. Prouty. Annabelle was talking about a Mr. Prouty who's going to sue her. Do you know him? Can you chin yourself? I can."

"No, I'm afraid I can't."

Raymond examined him with a critical eye. "You do look pretty weak. Why don't you take cod-liver oil if you like it so well?"

"I didn't say I liked it."

"Why didn't you take a drink when Iams offered you one?"

"I didn't want one, that's why."

"Major Fosdick-Browne drinks all the time. Annabelle says he's a sponge. Don't you drink?"

"Certainly I drink."

"Well," Raymond said, "I never saw anybody else around here turn down any liquor before." He produced a revolting-looking piece of candy from his pocket and put it in his mouth. "Major Fosdick-Browne has a cork leg," he said. "I jabbed him with the point of my compass and he didn't even notice."

"Isn't it near your bedtime?" William asked.

Raymond did not reply; other matters now claimed his attention. Taking a silver cigarette box from the table, he got down on his knees and began to push the box around the room, the while making unpleasant noises with his lips and tongue, as though to suggest the sounds of an improperly functioning automobile. "How did you know my name, anyway?" he said, looking up.

"A little bird told me."

"Yeh?" Raymond said. "Don't give me that crap."

William recoiled at this language. It was all too evident that Raymond could do with a tutor. He wondered, though, if he were the one for the job. It was not an appealing prospect. Raymond was endeavoring to tear off the top of the cigarette box at the hinge when Mrs. Diego Shanahan, garbed in a dress of violent green, came into the room.

"Raymond, put that back on the table this instant!" she commanded. "Why, Mr. Clay, what a surprise! So nice of you to come over. Raymond, have you been behaving yourself and showing Mr. Clay a nice time?"

Abandoning the box, Raymond got up and roamed about the room with a preoccupied air, ceaselessly rearranging and disturbing things.

"He's such a boy! So active! Did you meet Mr. Stokes?" she asked, sitting down beside William. "I think you'd enjoy talking with him, since he taught for a time himself. At some odd school or other in China. You wouldn't believe the things that went on there! I can't recall just now what it was he taught, but it sounded very interesting when he was telling us about it the other night. It made me realize that teaching could be terribly fascinating—taking some undisciplined but alert mind like Raymond's, for instance, and molding it, shaping it, watching it grow and unfold. Goodness, it's raining again! I'm sure we shall have more trouble with the drains in the cellar."

In a dark corner of the room, Raymond held a priceless folio volume of hand-tooled leather which he had taken from a shelf. Looking cautiously about to make sure he was hidden from view, he opened the book and allowed a plentiful amount of saliva he had been collecting to fall from his mouth onto the opened pages. Then he closed the book quietly and returned it to its proper place.

"Raymond! What are you doing back there! Come here at once!" Mrs. Shanahan said. When he came out and stood before her, an innocent look in his eyes, she patted him rather absently on the head and asked, "Now, aren't you ashamed of what you did to Modigliani this afternoon? After all, he is a living creature and has feelings like anyone else."

"I didn't hurt him," Raymond said, twisting away from her and kicking at a corner of the rug.

"You hurt him very much indeed, Raymond. The veterinarian had never seen anything like it. I am sure Modigliani has never harmed you in any way."

"Ah, nuts," said Raymond.

"Now run to Iams and let him take you up to bed! Say goodnight to Mr. Clay, dear."

"I don't want to go to bed!"

"But you must, dear. You must be bright and fresh for tomorrow."

"I don't want to go to bed! Raymond threw himself on the floor and rolled over and over, kicking animatedly.

"Raymond! Get up this instant!" Mrs. Shanahan rang for Iams. "Would you mind seeing if you can do anything with him, Mr. Clay? I don't know why he must carry on like this. Careful he doesn't bite you."

William was saved from this dangerous undertaking by the prompt arrival of Iams. Iams employed what appeared to be a modified version of jiu-jitsu to get Raymond upstairs, although the boy succeeded in ripping his tie and shirtfront rather badly before he had him under control. A number of feathers from Raymond's Indian suit were strewn about the floor.

"Do sit down, Mr. Clay!" Mrs. Shanahan said. "I don't know why it is, but Raymond always seems to be particularly high-spirited just at this time of evening. I should hate to have you think he's like this all the time. He's my sister's child, you know. His father was very headstrong and intractable; the whole family were that way, as a matter of fact." She toyed with one of her earrings. "I believe you know that I'm taking Raymond to Buenos Aires for the winter and that I'm looking for a tutor for the little fellow. Now, tell me, are you definitely interested?"

"Well," William said, "it would depend."

"Of course, of course. I really think you would do very well, although I'm not sure that you have had sufficient experience in handling children. A child with Raymond's temperament often requires a very firm and steady hand, an experienced hand. That's one reason why I thought perhaps two persons would be necessary, and I'm terribly sorry that Dorothy has finally decided that she isn't going to go."

"I beg your pardon?"

"Oh, didn't you know? She was over this afternoon and told me she can't consider it now. That horrible man she was married to who wouldn't give her a divorce died, you know. In a hospital here this morning. Terrible thing. Concussion of the brain. Some barroom disturbance he was in, I believe. Well, now, of course, Dorothy's free—free as a bird, and some man I don't know the slightest thing about has talked her into marrying him and going out to California. She seems to be crazy about him. Don something. You ought to go down and say good-bye to her before she leaves, because I think she was really quite fond of you, but you'll have to hurry because they were planning to get away about eight-thirty and it must be—"

Above them a great commotion broke out. One of the maids began to scream from the upstairs hall and Iams was calling to Mrs. Shanahan from the head of the stairs.

William followed her as she hurried into the hall.

"For Heaven's sake, what is it, Iams?"

"It's little Raymond, ma'am. He has fallen out of the window."

"Oh my God."

"Purcell has gone down to get him. He thinks both of his arms are broken."

"Oh my God."

They went out the front door, followed by Mr. and Mrs. Stokes and the Fosdick-Brownes. Purcell, one of the servants, came around the side of the house in the rain, carrying Raymond.

"He isn't dead, is he?" Mrs. Shanahan demanded, breathing heavily. "Oh, thank Heavens, he could have been killed. Reginald, go call the doctor!" she said to Fosdick-Browne. "Tell Iams to call Dr. Funk. What was he doing, Purcell? How did he fall out of the window, in God's name?"

"He was throwing rocks at some passersby, I believe, ma'am," Purcell said respectfully, carrying Raymond into the house.

"Oh my God, oh my God," was all Mrs. Shanahan could say. The little group stood about in bewildered attitudes for several moments before they realized how hard the rain was coming down. Mrs. Stokes, still carrying her cards, put her arm around Mrs. Shanahan and guided her into the house.

The others followed. Major Fosdick-Browne, having called Dr. Funk, headed for the liquor and poured himself a stiff drink. After downing it, he poured another for Mrs. Shanahan. The others helped themselves. William stood just inside the door. The pale woman kept saying, "Dreadful, dreadful." The servants could he heard dashing about upstairs.

"Naturally," said Mrs. Shanahan, dropping into a chair, "the Buenos Aires trip is quite out of the question now."

When he could do so conveniently, William offered his condolences and left. He drove back to the Hotel Riggs. The only person in the lobby was a boy who ran the elevator at night.

"No, she checked out about an hour ago," he said. "Some guy came for her in his car. I brought them

down in the elevator. She had a funny line and she
was carrying a bowl of goldfish. She kept saying to
this guy, 'Now are you sure that doctor in Los Angeles
can straighten your eyes, Don?' She called him Don
. . . He seemed to be worried about finances and
she told him he didn't need to worry because some
girl she knew had just paid her back some money
she'd loaned her a long time ago . . . No, she didn't
leave no forwarding address."

E I G H T E E N

The window was open only a few inches, but it
was growing cold in the room. William got up and
closed it and stood looking out at the street. Mr.
Esterling was walking back and forth in front of the
house with the dog.

In a second-floor room of the house next door, a
girl was undressing. She was rather plump and wore
an unironed slip. William wondered if she could
be the one who played the Czerny. It was not
unfeasible. These days she was moving on to *The
March of the Jolly Goblins.* He watched her perform-
ing reducing exercises for a while and then he came
away from the window and looked again at a piece
of paper on his desk.

Dear Frances, You cannot imagine how great the pres-

*sure of work has been here. Forgive me for taking so
long to write, but I have been*

He dotted an *i* he had missed and then slowly
tore up the letter and threw the pieces in the wastebasket.

"Telephone, Mr. Clay!" Mrs. Esterling called.

"Coming."

He went downstairs and picked up the telephone,
removing from the chair a red rubber object shaped
like a bone, with which the dog sometimes amused
itself.

"Hello," he said.

It was Devlin. "Bill, can you come down to the
railroad station right away? I'm catching a train
that leaves in half an hour."

"What happened?"

"Tell you when I see you."

"I'll start now."

He found Devlin in the bar. He was looking
unusually spruce.

"You made record time," Devlin said, breaking off
a conversation he was having with a genial Moor-
ish-looking man who carried a gold-headed cane.
"I didn't know whether I'd catch you at home or
not."

"I'm there most of the time now."

A waitress came over and glared down at them.

"Have one of these?" Devlin said, tapping his finger
against his glass.

"I don't mind if I do."

"Another," Devlin said to the waitress. "What did you mean by that remark?" he asked William.

"What remark?"

"That you're at home most of the time?"

"Well, Dorothy's gone, you see."

"Oh."

"To California. Last week."

"Rather sudden, wasn't it?"

"Pretty sudden."

"This departure of mine is something of a rush order, too."

"Leaving for good?"

"Didn't I tell you that the Mizpah boys always come through? Never catch them napping. Had a wire this afternoon. The South again, a boy's school. It seems I'm expected to teach wind instruments, among other things, but I like the climate down there, wonderful climate, especially with winter coming on. And beggars cannot be choosers."

"Do you know wind instruments?"

"Haven't the faintest idea about them."

"What will you do?"

"To tell you the truth, I've scarcely given it a thought. The Mizpah boys will tell them anything, you know."

The waitress brought William's drink. The Moorish gentleman was grinning at them, showing his gold teeth.

"Pretty soon now," he said to Devlin.

"Where's your wife?" William asked.

"Well, you know, Bill, I had rather good luck there. Remarkably good luck. As things worked out, I didn't have to give her that stock after all."

"How did you manage it?"

"In a strange manner."

"What do you mean?"

"Well, I'll tell you. I introduced her to Melvin Cathcart Lund."

"And they took to each other?"

"They're inseparable, simply inseparable."

A small, undistinguished man in a dark suit peered in the door as though searching for someone. He nodded timidly to Devlin.

"Hello, Boepple," Devlin said.

The man was gone.

"Is that Mordecai Boepple?" William asked.

"That's him."

"The reason I asked—I didn't think he'd look like that. I thought he'd be more—well, distinguished."

"Mordecai Boepple? Why, he's about the most colorless, commonplace person I've ever known. Totally without distinction in every way."

"Why is it," said William, "that people are always talking about him all the time?"

"Talking about him all the time? You must be feverish. Why in God's name would anyone want to talk about Mordecai Boepple? I can't ever remember anyone talking about him."

"Remember that night we went to Miss McVetchen's? Well, she was talking about him."

"Miss McVetchen?"

"She mentioned him a number of times."

"Did she?" said Devlin. He was losing interest. "What time is it?" he asked the Moor.

"Couple of minutes now. I go on platform."

"See you there."

"Righto." He went out.

"She talked about him a great deal. And that girl— the one whose father destroyed her scholarship?"

"Bessie Llewelyn."

"Yes. She talked about him. Everyplace I've gone here they talked about him."

"Christ," said Devlin under his breath. "What dull times, what dull times." In the distance a whistle sounded and they finished their drinks. "Well, this looks like it. My new-found friend, that dusky gentleman, claims to be a master of the French horn. He's going to show me a thing or two about wind instruments on our journey."

"Wish you weren't going," William said.

"New vistas," Devlin said. He put on his hat and picked up a suitcase covered with cracked and peeling labels. "New vistas beckon me, William. The open road, new worlds to conquer, the French horn to be reckoned with, the age-old call of adventure and romance."

They went out to the platform. The train was pulling

in. Devlin put out his hand. "Well, so long, kid. I
may be going to a smaller salary and a quinine climate, but my spirit—" Steam had begun to engulf
them. "The Guthrie School, Lobo, Alabama, will
reach me."

"Good-bye."

Devlin was on the train. He stood for a moment
on the steps smiling at William. The bell began to
ring. Devlin and the Moor were waving to him from
a window. He watched the light on the observation
car disappearing down the tracks and then he walked
back to his car.

NINETEEN

Toward the close of the year, Nelson Castleman
brought out a volume called *The Boy's Book of Handi-
craft*, Ingrid Spitalnick severed her connection with
the Communist Party and developed an interest in
the study of Hindu philosophy, and Chester Thompson
won third prize in a competition for a mural to be
placed in the Governor's office, receiving a medal
that later tarnished.

William saw none of them, however, and once
crossed the street to avoid speaking to Ingrid Spitalnick. No word came from Devlin, but he had a
note from Dr. Gormley, who regretfully informed

him that publication of his thesis had been indefinitely postponed due to circumstances beyond his
control. For a short time afterwards, William suffered from slight facial eruptions and from odd ringing
noises in his left ear. He let his car go back to the
dealer and began to exercise in the gymnasium, where,
twice a week, he threw a heavy ball about, wearing
a white outfit that was too large for him. He cut
down on his smoking and each night swallowed two
tablespoons of a bitter-tasting tonic which a physician had recommended. Coming upon Dr. Showers
in the hall one day, he was addressed in a manner
delicately bordering on approval. He did not know
what was intended by such an approach.

In December he accepted an invitation, which
coincided with the improvement of his complexion,
to join Upsilon Delta, a discussion club organized
by some of the younger faculty men.

One night, coming home through a wet snow from
one of their meetings, which had been held that evening
at the home of an assistant professor of animal
husbandry, and where an interesting paper, "Is
Humanism a Living Force?" had been read, William
passed the bar of the Hotel Bryant, hesitated for a
moment, and then went in.

The place was nearly deserted. He ordered a beer.
As he waited for the foam to settle, someone put a
nickel in the jukebox and it began to play the rec-

ord he had heard when he had first come in, his
first evening in town.

> *You're my thrill,*
> *You do something to me,*
> *Send the chills right through me,*
> *When I look at you I can't sit still:*
> *You're my thrill.*

A terrible nostalgia sifted over him. Now he could
not even recall distinctly what she had looked like.
It was all beginning to fade. It struck him suddenly
that she had never sung for him; it was only on the
radio that he had heard her voice. Even on the night
that she had sung for the others at Mrs. Shanahan's,
he had been driving about in the rain. His eyes became faintly moist and he left without finishing his
beer. If only he had salvaged something, he thought—
a flower, a photograph, anything at all.

A few days later he telephoned Mrs. Shanahan from
his office to see if she might be persuaded to sell
her painting of Dorothy. She was not there; she
had gone East. No, Iams had gone, too, the colored
maid told him. Did Mrs. Shanahan have that painting of the girl that had hung in the den? William
asked. No, that was gone, the maid said; shortly
after his arms were out of their casts, little Raymond
had taken it from the wall and defaced it so thor-

oughly that Mrs. Shanahan had been forced to burn it.

William thanked her and went down the hall to his ten o'clock class. The odor in the hall had become much more pronounced of late and it was rumored that something definite was to be done about it before the year was over. He opened the classroom door and sat at his desk as the last bell rang. Today they would take up the study of the essay, beginning with examples by Nicholas Murray Butler and David Starr Jordan.